THE
STORY
OF
LORA

Yvonne James 2016

First published in the United States of America by
The Willis Group

Copyright © 2016 by Yvonne Smith James
All rights reserved.

All rights reserved. No part of this publication may be reproduced, distributed, or transmitted in any form or by any means, including photocopying, recording, or other electronic or mechanical methods, without the prior written permission of the publisher, except in the case of brief quotations embodied in critical reviews and certain other noncommercial uses permitted by copyright law.

For more information, or to contact Yvonne Smith James, please visit www.StoryofLora.com

ISBN 13: 978-0-692-76615-6

The Story of Lora is a work of fiction. Names, characters, places, and incidents are the products of the author's imagination or are used fictitiously. Any resemblance to actual events, locales, or persons, living or dead, is entirely coincidental.

Printed in the United States of America

REVIEWS

"*The Story of Lora* has a brilliantly developed narrative with qualities to go immediately from print to film. This story captures your every emotion. I laughed, I cried and I eagerly anticipated every chapter. It will be the topic of conversation long after you have finished reading it."

—*Fitzroy Willis, MA, MS, PhD, The Willis Group, LLC*

"I found *The Story of Lora* engaging and a wonderful read. The book is a captivating portrait of relationships, with a backdrop of several social issues that are real and of concern in today's time. It is a story of the human spirit and it is one that leaves you wanting to learn more about the characters. Hopefully, there will be a sequel."

—*Rosa L. Jones, DSW, LCSW, Founding Faculty & Vice President Emerita of Student Affairs, Florida International University*

"A solid and impressive work, especially for a first time novelist. *The Story of Lora* is shaped by absorbing themes that are rooted deeply in black American experience. Vivid scenes, characters and dialogue provide material that could easily be adapted for the big screen. Lora is a welcome addition to our popular culture! We need more diverse main characters in our novels and movies… Why not start with portraying compelling black female protagonists more often in the stories we consume?"

—*Dr. Mark Rennella, Editor, Harvard Business Publishing*

"*The Story of Lora* relates an incredibly powerful story of vulnerability and invisible injustice that often times unknowingly surrounds us. We are drawn into the story where Lora is able to extend unbelievable forgiveness to others, while she struggles to forgive herself. It's a remarkable and challenging story."

—*Gloria Dingeldein, Associate Director, Florida International University*

APPRECIATION

My friend, Gloria Dingeldein

My friend, Dr. Rosa Jones

My Harvard professor, Dr. Mark Rennella

My editor, Adam Robinson, Good Book Developers

My son-in- law, Dr. Fitzroy Willis

DEDICATION

To My Mother
Your spirit has been with me from the very first
to the very last word written.

To My Father
You always made me feel special. I hope my
writing this book will make you proud.

To My Children
You are my greatest blessings.

To My Grandchildren
May all your dreams come true!

She spoke to me and told me about her life. There were days when she was reluctant to talk with me, but I persisted. And there were days when I did not understand her, but I was patient. After she finished telling me her story, I knew it was a story that others would want to hear.

—YSJ

THE STORY OF LORA

CHAPTER 1

The Neighborhood

Danny was deep in his studies when he heard the rumbling truck approaching and he peered out the window. It pulled up to the house that had been vacant and up for sale for nearly two years. Weeds had grown up as high as sugar cane, while rats scurried along the rooftop through the gutters, making their way into and out of the little house that sat in the middle of the neighborhood cul-de-sac. Windows had been boarded up to keep out the *hood rats*—squatters, crack heads, homeless—who came from the undesirable part of the town just a half mile away. But they still made their way in as easily as the roof rats. This was probably a major reason why the house stayed on the market for so long.

It was the end of winter, just shortly before spring 1980, when the *For Sale* sign came down and the nailed up slats of plywood were removed from the windows. Danny, the only kid in the neighborhood, as well as the rest of the neighbors, were more anxious for the house to be sold than the realtors waiting for their commission. The place had become an eyesore, and, with the hood rats, a safety concern as well.

"Ma, Ma, a U-Haul is here! A car just pulled up too. I think it's the new neighbors," Danny shouted. Edna turned the stove burner down to low and joined her son at the window. The movers exited the truck and a figure dressed in a floppy straw hat, long sleeve shirt and overalls exited the car.

"Who is that, in the hat?" Danny asked. Days earlier, when the realtor was there to take down the *For Sale* sign, Edna inquired about the buyer, and was told that it was a widowed lady with two children.

"I am guessing it's the new owner. And it looks like those are her two children now getting out of the car," Edna observed.

"Where is the father?" Danny inquired further.

"Dead, I was told," Edna answered.

"That's sad," Danny said as he watched the two little girls and the lady in the hat walk from the driveway and enter the house. "Maybe I should go over there and see if they need some help unloading," Danny suggested.

"No, that's the movers' job. Besides, you need to get back to studying for that big exam if you want to get into the pre-collegiate programs next semester. Edna realized she too had better get back to the pot of potatoes slowly cooking on the stove.

The Neighborhood

• ◆ •

Lora Jones made a vow to herself that in spite of not having the help of a husband, her twin daughters would have a nice home to live in. The apartment that she had been living in for the past four years was not what she had envisioned, and it was barely what she could tolerate. She wanted to live in a decent neighborhood, with nice people, where she and her girls would feel safe—unlike like the apartment where the smell of marijuana, cigarettes and alcohol permeated the narrow corridors, and vagabonds lurked in the alley. She wanted a home where she could enjoy peace and tranquility, rather than hearing voices and noises from surrounding neighbors that vibrated through the paper thin walls.

Lora wanted a home with a yard where she could plant flowers and her girls could run around and play, rather than a sidewalk where children would jump rope and play hop scotch next to a busy street with passing cars fumigating the air with the smell of exhaust.

It did not matter how fancy the house was or if it had all the bells and whistles of modern day homes. Also, she realized that the bank would only approve her for a modest loan, which narrowed her choices to a very few that were available in this area of Augusta, Georgia.

This house spoke to Lora with its quiet charm and potential. She was confident that she could make it look as nice as those she saw in the glossy home-sale brochures, even with her limited finances. The only thing she was not sure of was the neighbors—what kind of people were they? The realtor told her that they were law abiding and mostly older people. "Mature as the tall oak trees in the neighborhood," the realtor described them.

Lora was also concerned about her neighbors accepting her. She was quite the introvert, but she did like people and she wanted people to like her and—more importantly—for them to like her children. She was not concerned that there were no other young children in the neighborhood. The girls would be attending their same school, where they had plenty of friends, and there was a nearby park and playground for children.

As they entered the house, Lora turned to her girls with a smile and asked, "Well, little ladies, how do you like your new home?" Although they were fraternal twins, with distinctive looks and personalities, they often spoke and answered questions in unison.

"It looks kinda dirty, and there's holes in the wall. Yeah, and it smells funny too. Stinky."

"Well, let's get rid of that stinky smell," Lora replied as she started opening windows. "Go away, stinky smell! Get out of our house!" Lora said while

The Neighborhood

flapping her hands as if she were shooing the smells out of the window.

"Yeah, yeah, go away, stinky smell!" the girls shouted as they imitated their mother.

Lora had hoped for a more positive reaction from the girls when they saw their new home, but then she realized they were too young to see or understand its potential. Most likely they expected the inside to look like the inside of the apartment that had been the only place they'd known since age two. While the slum apartment had its faults, Lora had decorated the inside to look bright, cozy and comfortable and was careful to not let the girls see disturbing things that went on outside of their apartment.

With the smell of fresh air pervading the house, Lora attempted to further assure the girls. "Mommy is going to fix everything up, and when I'm done, we'll have the most beautiful house in the neighborhood. And do you know where we are going to start? Your bedroom! Come with me, my little soldiers." She marched the girls to their bedroom.

Much to her surprise, the room was clean and in good condition compared to the rest of the house. Its two large windows faced east, which invited the morning sunshine in. Lora liked this because she used to have to tell her six-year-old, sleepy, I-don't-wanna-get-up girls, "Mr. Sunshine is up and waiting for you!" In the slum apartment it was only an imaginary sunshine because there were no windows in their bedroom.

Lora's imagination and ideas on how to decorate the room went into high gear, and so did the girls'. "I want my bed here. And I want mine right here. We can paint this wall red, this one green, this one blue and this one orange. Yay! And the curtains are going to be purple with pink and white polka dots. Yay! And we want a bright yellow door to look like Mr. Sunshine. Yay! And we can put stars on the ceiling to look like night. Yay!" While the girls' visions (with the exception of the stars on the ceiling) were a far cry from what Lora was envisioning, she was delighted over their now positive spirit.

"Okay, ladies, now let me show you your bathroom—your own bathroom—that you don't have to share with Mommy." She took them to the bathroom just off their room, opened the door and was greeted by a family of scattering cockroaches. Lora slammed it shut before the girls got a glance of the unwelcome house guests.

"On second thought, let's get to work on your bedroom," she said as she hurriedly redirected the girls back to their room.

The movers had been kind enough to place all the furniture and labeled boxes in their respective rooms for no extra charge. The only major things Lora had to do in the girls' room were to assemble the twin beds and unpack their boxes. "I want you two ladies to start unpacking your clothes and put them in the dresser drawers, and put your shoes in the closet. Clothes that need to be hung up, put them on hangers. Let Mommy hang them in the closet because the rod is too high for you." Lora made a mental note to have another rod installed lower so that they could reach it.

Lora knew that the girls would probably only complete a fraction of what she assigned, and she'd probably have to redo most of it if it were to be done properly. But it didn't matter. What mattered was that they were engaged and taking pride in fixing up their room.

As the girls were busy doing what they had been instructed, Lora's mind went to the bathroom.

"And while you're unpacking, Mommy has some business to do in the bathroom."

"You have to pee pee, Mommy?" Cecilia asked.

"No," Lora answered chuckling, but also thinking seriously that the girls would have to go soon and the urgency of cleaning the roach motel.

As Lora rifled through the boxes for roach spray and cleaning supplies, she came across the box marked *radio/cassette tapes*.

"How about some music!" she shouted to the girls.

"Yay!" the girls gleefully replied.

"What do you want to hear, little ladies?"

In unison they answered, "Whatever makes you happy, Mommy."

Tears of joy filled Lora's eyes as she said to herself, "Your happiness is what makes me happy." She found a cassette with Alvin and The Chipmunks' songs, set it to play and hurried back to clean the bathroom.

It was an opportune time for the move. Lora had two weeks of vacation time. From dawn until the late hours of the night, Lora worked feverishly and tirelessly.

She made her *Things To Do* list. Her first priority was to get rid of the roof rats and any other roaches, which she had negotiated at the closing to be done prior to moving in and to be paid for by the sellers. She called and complained to them. Just two hours after she hung up the phone, the exterminating service was there and took care of the problem—the rats and roaches—and gave her a three-month warranty.

Her second priority was to secure the doors and windows to keep the hood rats out. With the high costs quoted to her by locksmiths, she decided to do it herself and purchased top quality, guaranteed locks and followed the installation guides. She thought about how nice it would be to have an alarm system, but that was something she would have to put on her wish list.

Her third priority was to cut down the sugar cane-tall weeds and tree branches that engulfed the house, and to cut the grass. She hired a company that was referred to her by the nursery where she worked. To cut her lawn on a regular basis, they offered her a discount because of her affiliation with the nursery: $20 per cut. She did not have the time or equipment to maintain the yard, so she accepted the offer. She crossed out the priorities on her *Things to Do* list, and proceeded to the things that she had an affinity for—the décor.

She wanted the exterior painted but did not have enough funds, nor was she able to tackle it herself because of the height. So, she settled on hiring a company to pressure wash the stucco, roof and driveway—hoping that a good cleaning would suffice. Her own physical efforts went toward fixing up the interior.

She patched the holes in the walls and painted every room, nook and cranny, including the ceilings. As the carpet installers were removing the worn and stained carpet in the living and dining rooms, she looked at the natural dark oak wood floors underneath and thought it was a shame that something so beautiful would be covered up. She opted to have only the bedrooms re-carpeted. She refinished the living and dining room herself by sanding down the wood planks and bringing back the natural wood with coats of varnish. "It may not be what's in style," she thought, "but it's what I like and this is my home, and I'm the one who has to live here." The kitchen and bathrooms were good for the time being with vinyl flooring, which she scrubbed deeply.

Because the house did not have air conditioning, she had ceiling fans installed throughout. Also, the house did not come with a stove, fridge, washer or dryer, but she was able to save by buying discontinued models rather than the new, expensive, state of the art models. She had always wanted a dishwasher, but that was something else she would have to put on her wish list along with the alarm system and central air. She did, however, go over budget with the purchase and installation of a mahogany door with a sculptured oval glass window. She could not resist it.

The room that Lora most enjoyed working on was the girls' room. While the room was not quite decorated as the girls envisioned, they did get their yellow door, purple curtains and the silver glittered ceiling that simulated stars. "Yay!" they shouted as Lora completed the final custom touch—the girls' names in wooden block letters above their beds. Lora had painted the letters in their favorite colors—red for Cecilia, and blue for Veronica. The collage of colors was not to Lora's liking, but it was close to what the girls envisioned and made them happy.

On Sunday morning, the day before Lora was scheduled to return to work, she received a housewarming present. Her co-workers came over with plants and flowers and two pallets of grass and landscaped her yard. One thing they planted in her backyard was a peach tree that was in its infancy. "If you're a true Georgia girl, you gotta have a peach tree," they said, smiling. They also gave her a bottle of wine. "It's an expensive vintage, you might want to keep it for a special occasion." Lora was appreciative of the wine, but she did not drink—not even on special occasions.

That Sunday evening, after her kind co-workers left and the girls had retired, Lora put the bottle of wine in her china cabinet, flopped down on the sofa and realized how exhausted she was. But her exhaustion could not outweigh her happiness, and she was proud of what she accomplished in just two weeks. She took her *Things To Do* list out of her overalls and checked off *Landscaping, $100.*

As she looked at the list, she realized one thing she had completely forgotten. She wrote it down, and marked it priority—*Meet my new neighbors.*

CHAPTER II

The Neighbors

SPRING HAD SPRUNG AND SO HAD THE LITTLE house in the middle of the cul-de-sac. While the house still had cracks in its stucco exterior, cement walkway and driveway, the good pressure cleaning took care of the cobwebs and dirt. It also brought back the original color of ivory stucco, brown trim and shingles and gray concrete. A tapestry of yellow, blue, pink and purple flowers and fresh Zoysia grass, that her co-workers had planted, brought life to the house and made it look inviting. The two oak trees on each side of the house had been immaculately cut and shaped as well. Lora thought they looked majestic, like the stoic Queen's Guard standing on each side of the entrance to Buckingham Palace. While the richness of the mahogany door, embellished by its oval beveled glass and brass door handle and lock, seemed incongruent with the plain stucco and nondescript tile roof, it was not pretentious. Rather, it made the house look warm and inviting.

◆ ◆ ◆

Friendships between Lora and her neighbors also began to bloom that spring.

"Mama J, Mama J, you there?" Edna called out as she rang the doorbell to the neighbor next door to her.

"I'm coming!" Mrs. Johnson, affectionately known as Mama J, had lived in the neighborhood longer than anyone. Before that, she lived where the hood rats now congregated. She moved into this neighborhood when the "white folks fled because of too many black folks moving in," she would explain.

"How you doing, Ms. Edna? Come on in."

"Boy, it smells good in here. Whatcha cooking?" asked Edna, sniffing, as she followed Mama J into the kitchen.

"A big pot of collard greens with ham hocks, and an apple pie." She opened the oven door to check on the almost-done pie—golden crisp, bubbling juice oozing up through the slits in the crust.

One might describe Mama J as a stereotypical grandmother. She usually dressed in a floral pastel house dress and house slippers, and wore her salt and pepper hair neatly tied back in a bun. But on Sundays, as she put it, "I dress for the Lord." Her attire then consisted of brocade and silk two-piece maxi-length suits, and support weight knee-high stockings with comfortable yet stylish one-inch pumps. The night before church, she would let down her bun and roll the ends of her hair with makeshift rollers made from paper bags. The next morning, after she put on her clothes, she would top the salt and pepper curls cascading down her shoulders with a wide brimmed hat decorated with silk flowers and ribbon. Clutching her Bible, she then walked a quarter of a mile to the church that she had attended for the past 20 years to worship the Lord.

Mama J's favorite pastimes were quilt making and tending to her little vegetable garden, where she grew collard greens and tomatoes. She never missed her appointments with Jesus—one hour with her Bible first thing in the morning, and one hour in the evening shortly before she retired. The highlight of her week, other than church, were the weekends when she would cook for her children and grandchildren. They would visit twice a month.

Edna opened the lid to the pot of greens, hoping that they had been cooking long enough for her to get a taste. She commented, "Looks like you're cooking for your children and grandkids this weekend."

"Nope, not this weekend, Ms. Edna. Cookin' for our new neighbor. She's been here nearly three weeks, and all we have done is give her a wave. Plannin' on making a visit this Saturday."

Edna, feeling reprimanded because she hadn't made any effort to welcome the new neighbor, replied, "Well, I figured she didn't want to be bothered. She's so quiet. Never makes no attempt to introduce herself. Heck, you can't even see what she looks like, always wearing that big floppy hat and overalls."

Mama J practiced and preached traditional southern hospitality. "It's not her obligation to introduce herself to us. It's ours. Courtesy as neighbors. Nowadays, people live next to each other for years and don't even know each other's name. Never even speak to one another. I think that's a pity and a shame. When someone knocks on your door, you open it. If you want them to come in, you say 'welcome, please come in.' Same thing with a new neighbor. Them moving is like knocking on the door. Us neighbors supposed to open that door and say welcome to the neighborhood."

Edna tried to redeem herself with compliments about their new neighbor. "She has done quite a nice job over there, especially considering she doesn't have a man. Ooh, and that mahogany front door she put in, I want me one. And those little girls—they are so cute and seem so well-behaved. Never see them running around or screaming like your—"

"Like my grandchildren, when they come over?" Mama J interjected. "Don't look apologetic, Edna. The truth is the truth." Both ladies chuckled.

The Neighbors

Even though the collard greens were not quite done, Edna dipped into the pot with a fork and took a steaming hot mouthful. While fanning her mouth to relieve the sting from the heat, Mama J teasingly asked her, "They hot enough? I mean the pepper?" Mama J giggled as Edna took a napkin and patted her mouth and eyes that were watering from the heat sting, and giggled as well.

When her mouth was soothed, Edna continued with observations about their new neighbor. "Doesn't seem like she has any family or friends either. Never see anyone visiting her. I don't think she even goes to church."

"All the more reasons we should introduce ourselves—let her know she can count on us as neighbors. I spoke to Big Lucy. She's bringing some potato salad."

"What about Milky? You know Big Black Lucy don't like her albino husband around any other women, maybe except you," Edna quipped.

"I wish you would stop calling him an albino, Edna. He's just light skinned. And you should stop calling her Big *Black* Lucy. Just calling her *Big* is kinda mean too."

"Okay, okay, Mama J, but you know it's true." Both women laughed as they knew their good-natured name calling was humorous rather than spiteful.

"And, oh, what about Mr. Felix? He is part of the neighborhood," Edna said.

"No way!" snapped Mama J. "That cranky old man thinks he's better than everybody in the neighborhood—in the whole country even—always talking about how great Jamaica is, like his dookie don't stink. Why don't he just take his cranky, snooty self back there if it's so great?"

Edna, amused, said "Why listen to you name callin'. Didn't you tell me I shouldn't be doing that?"

"Yeah, but just ain't no kind words I can say about that man."

Edna, still amused and trying to further get Mama J's goat, replied, "Now, Mama J, you know you like that man. Y'all about the same age. I think you two would make a—"

"Edna, don't make me do something Jesus won't forgive," Mama J said, vexed, as she picked up a cooking spoon and pointed it toward Edna.

"Ah, woman, you know I'm just teasing. Where's your sense of humor?" Edna said as she chuckled under her breath. She then tried to say something that would appease Mama J.

"Well I'll partake in the visit by making some fried chicken. How's that?"

"Make some cornbread too, to go along with these collard greens. Need to be over there by six, men can stay home, just us ladies." Mama J said, still agitated at the thought of Mr. Felix.

"Bye, Mama J. I'll see you tomorrow," Edna said. As she walked back to her house, she again chuckled about how she got Mama J's goat.

The Neighbors

Earlier that week, Mama J wrote a note on her special stationery and put it in Lora's mailbox. It read:

Dear New Neighbor,

We would like to pay you a visit this coming Saturday at 6 pm to welcome you to the neighborhood and bring you dinner. To respond, you may use the enclosed RSVP card and put in my mailbox. Cordially, Mrs. Johnson, Mail Box 615.

Lora smiled when she read the invitation and thought, "How sweet." She responded, *I would be honored.*

Shortly before their anxiously awaited visit, the ladies made final preparations. Edna went over to get the pot of greens from Mama J, which was too heavy for Mama J to carry, and put it in the box alongside her fried chicken and corn bread. Big Lucy, in addition to the potato salad she had made that morning, decided at the last minute to make some chocolate chip peanut butter cookies. In the haste, she almost burned herself trying to plate them while they were still hot. Mama J put on her best house dress and a pair of her church shoes. At just a minute shy to 6, the ladies opened their doors and headed out on their mission to get to know their new neighbor, as if it were a pilgrimage.

"Got to get me one of these doors," Edna thought again as she admired the mahogany door. Mama J rang the brass doorbell. Lora opened it to their welcoming smiles.

"Hello, I am Mrs. Johnson, but everyone calls me Mama J."

"Lucy Babcock, pleasure to meet you."

"Edna Ayoka, but please just call me Edna."

"Nice to meet you all. My name is Lora Jones, just call me Lora. Please come in, ladies. These are my daughters, Cecilia and Veronica. Girls, what do you say?"

"Hello, nice to meet you, and welcome to our home." Their obviously rehearsed greeting was followed by a little curtsy which was amusing and endearing to the ladies, as well as Lora. Cecilia tugged at the Bohemian style dress that Lora bought for the occasion and whispered, "Mommy, can we go back to our room now and play?" Lora looked at the ladies and, with motherly understanding, nodded her head approvingly. "Okay, I will call you when dinner is served," Lora said. The girls scurried back to their private little haven with its silver glittered ceiling and purple curtains.

The ladies now had Lora's undivided attention as she led them into the kitchen. "Boy, everything smells so good. It's been a long time since I had a good home cooked meal. These days it's usually McDonald's or frozen TV dinners," said Lora.

As the ladies followed her into the kitchen, they eyeballed everything in sight, and thoughts and questions entered into their heads. "Looks, smells like fresh paint; didn't see no workers going in to paint; did she do the painting herself? Nice drapes and curtains, wonder how much they cost? Furniture don't seem to match, French, modern, country—no tellin' what that is. Nice plants, all real? My artificial plants will do just fine. Got a lot of books, wonder if she has read them or are they just for show? That vase is unusual, wonder if it's antique, looks expensive. No photos except that one of the girls; that's odd. She's rather attractive without that floppy hat and overalls. Got that good hair too. Don't look pressed or permed. Kinda short though for my likin'."

As the ladies entered the small but bright kitchen, Lora instructed them to put everything anywhere they wanted. "The food is still warm and don't need to be heated up," advised Edna. The kitchen was too small to accommodate eating, so Lora invited them to sit in the dining room, which was adjacent to the living room. The ladies continued to follow her like tourists with Lora as their tour guide and their eyes the cameras as they focused on every detail. They noticed a china cabinet, but it had no china, only a bottle of wine. "Does she drink? Could she be an alcoholic?" they wondered. "Nah, don't look like one, don't act like one, seen enough to know one, but then you never know."

"Have a seat, ladies, wherever you like," Lora said trying to make the ladies feel comfortable. Each pulled out a chair, upholstered in dark green, seemingly linen fabric, and sat at the dark oak oval table for six. As Mama J inquired about where were the girls going to sit, Lora went into the small coat closet just beside the dining room and took out two child-size foldable chairs and the girls' tea party table that they had almost outgrown.

"On these. I was going to throw them out before I moved. Glad I didn't. Like they say, as soon as you throw something away, you find out you need it."

"I know that's right," Mama J said as the other ladies shook their heads in agreement.

In the middle of the table was a centerpiece made of an assortment of fresh flowers, a tray of deviled eggs and a tray of miniature meatballs stuck with toothpicks, and paper napkins. "Help yourselves, ladies, just some appetizers I made for this special evening." Because Lora was not sure what the ladies were bringing, and the girls were finicky eaters, she made an ample amount of meatballs, which she knew the girls would like.

"My husband, Milky, just loves deviled eggs," Lucy said as she tasted one of the morsels covered with a dash of paprika.

"Um, that's an unusual name," Lora said. "Is it a nickname, Ms. Lucy?"

"Nope, birth name. His parents are both as black as me."

Edna and Mama J looked at each other with the same surprised look and same thought: "Well I'll be! She calls her own self black!"

Lucy continued, "But somehow he came out light skinned. His daddy thought maybe he wasn't his, but the milkman's. So his daddy named him Milky—after the milkman and because he was so light skinned." Big Lucy picked up a meatball by its toothpick and continued. "Just so happened that while he turned out white as snow, his features were the spittin' image of his daddy—almost identical. Of course we know now—because us blacks are all mutts, so to speak—those recessive genes can come out at any time."

Edna looked befuddled, as did Mama J, and asked, "Why, Ms. Lucy, how come you never told me or Mama J about that?"

"Y'all never asked," she said nonchalantly as she popped another deviled egg in her mouth.

Lora found Big Lucy's frankness quite charming, and the story about Milky funny, but believable.

After setting up the girls' seating, Lora shouted out, "Girls, dinner is ready! Wash your hands and come immediately."

"Okay, Mommy!"

As the ladies were munching on the appetizers, the doorbell rang. Edna looked at Mama J and whispered, "Pray tell who is that?"

Lora wondered as well. "Are any other neighbors supposed to be coming, ladies?"

"No," the ladies answered in unison.

Lora walked from the dining room through the living room and small foyer and answered the door.

"Hello, my name is Danny. I'm Mrs. Ayoka's son from across the way."

"Nice to meet you, Danny. I am Mrs. Jones, Mrs. Lora Jones."

Danny, with a box in his hands, proceeded to say, "Well, I know my mother and the rest of the neighbors brought over some food. So I thought you might need some paper plates and plastic forks and spoons."

As he handed her the box, she replied, "Why that is very thoughtful of you. Would you like to come in and join us?"

"Oh no, no thank you. I'm working on a school project, but thank you anyway."

"School work on a Saturday night, that's impressive," Lora replied, disappointed that he couldn't stay. "I'll fix you a plate, and have your mother bring it over when she leaves."

Danny and Lora exchanged 'thank you' again and wished each other a good evening. In the meantime, all the ladies were stretching their necks to see, and straining their ears to hear, who was at the door. But the confines of the foyer did not allow them to see or hear. The ladies tried to conceal their curiosity when Lora returned. The girls, oblivious to everything, were enjoying the miniature meatballs but did not like the deviled eggs. They stabbed them with the toothpicks from the meatballs saying, "die monster, die."

Lora knew that the ladies were dying to know who was at the door, and she wanted to tease them with the suspense. So, as she returned, she looked at them sheepishly and said, "Ladies, I can tell you are all wondering who that was? Well, it was a very, very handsome young man." Now, the ladies were really titillated, and Lora intentionally prolonged the suspense with a few seconds of silence. Just as Big Lucy was about to say, "Get on with it, girl!" Lora laughed and relieved their curiosity. "It was a darling young man named Danny—your son, Ms. Edna." All the ladies looked at one another disappointed as if to say, "Oh shoot, that's who!" The women all laughed.

As Lora started taking the contents out of the box, she explained, "He brought some things so that I won't have to wash dishes tonight. Hope y'all don't mind eating off paper plates. As you can see, I don't have any china," and gestured toward the china cabinet. Again they laughed, but again they wondered about the wine as they looked at the china cabinet. "What about that"—Big Lucy was about to ask about the wine until she felt a hard kick under the table—a signal telling her to shut her month—from Mama J who abruptly interrupted her.

"Mmm, mmm, mmm. All us women in here, and none of us thought to bring paper plates." Mama J said as Big Lucy still wondered about the bottle of wine.

With the appetizers all gone and no longer thinking about the wine, Big Lucy demanded, "Well, can we please eat now?"

Lora replied, "I'll start fixing the—"

Mama J interjected, "Honey, that's not necessary, we all can serve ourselves. You just take care of the girls." When everyone was seated and ready to eat, Mama J insisted that grace be said first, as she looked at the girls who now had their mouths full.

The suspense of who was at the door, and Lora's sense of humor, put the ladies at ease. After dinner, Lora—with the insistence and assistance of Mama J—prepared the girls for bed. Meanwhile, Edna and Big Lucy took the liberty of cleaning up and made tea that Lora had anticipated by leaving a kettle on the stove along with tea bags, a sugar bowl, and cups on the kitchen counter. "Ms. Lucy, Ms. Edna, with the leftovers, can you please make a plate to take home to Danny, and your husbands as well?" Lora called from the girls' room. Edna and Lucy opted not to make plates for their husbands because they had prepared dinner for them before they left home. But Edna did make Danny a plate. At 15, he was eating like a horse.

After the girls were tucked in bed, and the paper plates discarded, the ladies gathered comfortably in the living room. While sipping on tea and

The Neighbors

munching on the homemade chocolate chip peanut butter cookies that Big Lucy had made, the ladies spent the next two hours getting to know their new neighbor.

Although Lora was a private person and did not easily share her personal business, that evening she confided in the ladies many things about her life. Perhaps this openness was because she needed someone to talk with, perhaps because she wanted the neighbors to like her, or perhaps it was because she found an immediate kindred spirit in them.

Contrary to what the ladies had thought, Lora was not a widow. Her husband had disappeared four years ago. She and her husband—who was Jamaican—moved from New York to Atlanta when the girls were two. He was offered a job as a sous chef at a major restaurant and at a salary much higher than he was being paid at the Jamaican family-owned restaurant he was working at in Brooklyn.

Just six months later, he suddenly disappeared. He had not come home one evening, nor did he show up for work the next day. She called everyone they knew, but to no avail. She called 911, the police department and the hospitals. Still nothing. So three days later she filed a missing person report.

Mama J, thinking about Mr. Felix, asked if perhaps he went back to Jamaica. Lora said she highly doubted it; he did not have any close relatives there, nor had he expressed any desire to live in Jamaica.

Big Lucy asked if perhaps he ran off to be with another woman. Lora said while that is what most people thought, in her heart of hearts she did not think so.

Edna asked how their marriage was before he disappeared. Lora said happy, very happy. Edna further asked if had he been involved with drugs or illegal activities, whereby something more sinister could have happened, such as him being murdered. Lora said no, that was the last thing she would have suspected—and no because he called her six months later.

"Child, why didn't you tell us that from the start!" Big Lucy exclaimed. "We thinking he's dead!"

"Sorry, I was just trying to give you details so you could understand what I went through," Lora said apologetically.

"We understand, and I am glad you feel comfortable enough with us to share all this. Go on, my child," Mama J said sympathetically.

Lora took a deep breath. "He said he was in Europe, he had no financial means to help me or the girls—and to get on with my life." Lora stopped talking, but the ladies were now perched up in their seats, leaning forward with expressions that begged to hear more. But Lora just sat there saying nothing.

The silence was broken when the ladies in unison exclaimed, "That's it?"

The Neighbors

"That's it," Lora replied. "He did not give me a chance to ask or say anything. He just hung up. And I haven't heard from him since."

Silence again filled the room, but this time it was the astounded ladies deep in thought. Big Lucy leaned back and crossed her arms over her heavily bosomed chest. Edna crossed her legs and bobbed her foot so hard one would have thought her shoe would go flying across the room. Mama J cupped her hands together and bowed her head as if she were in prayer.

The silence was broken when Mama J asked, "So then what did you do, Lora?"

"Got on with my life, like he said. The girls were not traumatized because they were only two. I left Atlanta when I got a job at a plant nursery in this town, found a nearby apartment that I could afford, and saved every penny so I could buy this nice house for me and the girls. And here I am."

"So, Lora, not knowing where he is, the court ain't gonna be able to make him pay child support. Do you realize that?" Mama J asked.

Lora nodded her head yes.

"What about family to help you?" Edna asked. Lora shared that she was adopted, but at 18 her relationship with her adoptive parents was severed, and she left home. This was one part of her life that she did not want to share details about, so she told the ladies, with all due respect to them, she did not want to discuss this any further. The ladies didn't mind too much because they were caught up with interest in the story about her husband.

"How about friends?" Big Lucy asked. Lora said she never had any close friends. The closest she had ever felt to friends were those she shared with her husband, but they were his friends more than hers.

"How do you feel about him now?" Edna asked.

Lora replied, "I was relieved to know that he wasn't dead. Now I just want to know why he left, and somehow I think I will someday. Until then, I refuse to fill my heart with anger or resentment. Am I waiting or thinking he'll come back to me? No. But I pray with all my heart he will someday come back for the sake of his daughters."

The final question asked by the ladies was, "Do you still love him?"

"I don't know. I don't know if I can answer that until I know the reason why he left me and the girls."

Her answer put the conversation about her husband to rest, much to Lora's relief. She asked the ladies if they would like more tea, and they all responded, "Yes, please."

For the rest of the evening, the ladies and Lora engaged in light-hearted conversation. Lora told them about her job—why she always dressed in the hat and overalls, and how working there enabled her to get plants and flowers and landscaping. But mostly they talked about Lora's house. The ladies learned that her eclectic decor—mismatching furniture—was not a style choice but a result of her having to shop at thrift stores because of her tight budget. Yes, she had painted the entire interior of the house by herself. The vase, which Edna had eyeballed, was a piece that she lucked upon at a garage sale. Yes, she had read all those books. She was an avid reader and some of her favorite authors were Henry James, James Baldwin and Toni Morrison, names of which none of the ladies had a clue. There were no photos on the wall because she had not had time to unpack them. This was not the truth, but Lora didn't want to explain, and she felt she had talked enough about herself. Mama J refrained from asking her about church. She felt Lora's strain from talking about her husband. Now was not the time. She would wait until the time was right.

"Woo, it's after 10!" exclaimed Big Lucy as she checked her watch. With that said, Lora thanked the ladies for coming, and everyone gave each other a hug and said goodnight. Lora handed Edna the plate of leftovers and asked her to please make sure to tell Danny how much she appreciated his thoughtfulness. She assured the ladies she would return their pots and bowls, which still contained leftovers. Lora waited at the door until the ladies made their way back into their houses.

As the ladies entered their houses and turned off their porch lights, Lora stood at her door momentarily, feeling a peacefulness as she looked into the quiet of the night at her surroundings—her new neighborhood.

    She then turned off her porch light and went to check on the girls, who were fast asleep. The night light and twinkles from the silver glittered ceiling allowed her to see their little heads peeping out from under the soft pink floral comforters. She gave both a quiet kiss, proceeded to the kitchen and put the leftovers in the fridge. As she washed the now empty pots she said to herself, "Thank God I don't have dishes to wash," which caused her to think of Danny. "What a nice young man."

◆ ◆ ◆

"I'm home!" Edna called out as she headed to the kitchen, flipped on the light and put Danny's plate on the countertop. She could hear the faint sound of the television coming from the family room and figured Walter was in there dozing off in the recliner as he usually did this time of night. "Walter!"

    "He's in the—" Danny started to say as he entered the kitchen.

    "I know," Edna interrupted.

    "How was the dinner and meeting?" Danny asked.

    "Quite nice, and that was very thoughtful of you to bring paper plates, for which our new neighbor told me to tell you thank you. She sent you this plate of leftovers."

He rubbed his palms together in anticipation. "That's good, because I'm hungry."

"You *always* hungry," she replied as she unwrapped the aluminum foil to warm the food. But then she decided not to because the container itself was still warm, and Danny was too anxious to wait as he grabbed a fork from the drawer.

"Well, tell me how things went. Do you like her? What about her children?" Sitting at the kitchen table, he filled his stomach with food while Edna filled his ears with a recap of the evening, to which Danny listened attentively.

"Very nice young lady...girls are six years old, very mannerly...no husband—kind of a complicated story—adult conversation...works at a plant nursery, why she dresses the way she does...painted whole inside of house by herself." Looking at Danny's empty plate, she asked, "Was the food good?"

"Yes, ma'am, delicious." Although his stomach was full, he still wanted to hear more.

"And do you know that Ms. Lucy said all black folks are mutts?" Edna said as she gave the table a pound with her fist.

"No, how's that?" he asked, bemused.

She went on to tell him about Big Lucy's story about Milky. "Well, I got news for her. You, me and your daddy are not mutts. We are full blooded Nigerians. Straight from the Motherland."

Danny wanted to laugh, but dared not make light of his mother's agitation. Their conversation ended as Walter woke up and yelled, "Edna, you home?"

Danny prepared for bed, turned off the light, and as he lay in bed, he laughed out loud about the story of Milky. Then he smilingly thought about what his mother told him about their new neighbor, and his meeting with her at the door—Mrs. Jones, Mrs. Lora Jones. It was the first time he had seen her close up and without the hat. His stomach started to feel strange. Could it have been the food, he wondered. No, it was something else. It did not hurt, but it was weird—something he had never felt before, something that he could not explain.

◆ ◆ ◆

Lora was the center of attention that night, and she would continue to be the center of attention in the neighborhood for many years to come—but not always in a good way.

CHAPTER III

Perceptions

SUMMER WAS APPROACHING AND CECILIA AND Veronica were looking forward to going to the day camp that they had attended in the previous two years. Lora, however, was worried about whether she had enough money to pay the registration fee. She had depleted all her savings, including the money that she normally saved for their summer camp, in order to fix up the house. If she could not afford the camp, an alternative would be to send them to a county-funded daycare facility allocated for lower income working mothers. She cringed at the thought because of the negative things she had been told about the care of the children who attended. She also did not want the stigma of being perceived as a welfare recipient.

Then she thought that she might be able to pull back on some expenses. It was hard for her to think of anything because she was frugal with just about everything. Then a light bulb went off in her head — the lawn service! It was costing her $20 every two weeks. She *could* mow the lawn herself, but she did not have, nor could she afford, a lawnmower. Another light bulb went off in her head. At the nursery they had a couple of old lawnmowers that they never used. She wondered if she could rent one from them. But that still would only cover about a quarter of the cost. Too bad, she thought, that she didn't have anything she could sell or pawn. Oh, but she did. She had her wedding ring. Why not; she never wore it anymore.

She checked with the manager at the nursery to see if she could rent one of the mowers. He said no, but she could have it because he needed the storage space. He also said he had an edger and weed eater that were sitting back there collecting dust. They were hers as well if she wanted them. She knew that he could probably sell these and get some money, and she knew he could be doing this for her out of pity. However, she was not going to let pride stand in her way. Her girls needed to go to summer camp. She thanked him and said she would pick up the mower, edger and weed eater on the following Saturday.

Pawning her wedding ring, however, was a difficult choice because of its sentimental value. The following Saturday, as she was heading out to the pawn shop, she grabbed her car keys that were sitting next to the vase on the credenza. And at that moment she felt like she had struck gold. The vase—it might be worth something. Edna said that it looked like an antique, expensive. So she took it and her wedding ring to the pawn shop.

While she had never pawned anything, common sense told her to keep a poker face—not to look desperate, and don't accept the pawnbroker's first offer. He first offered her $100 for the vase. Lora told him it was worth far more, and he needed to come up at least to $1,000. He said the best he could do was $300. She replied, for $400 he had a deal. He took the deal. Then she thought about the wedding ring, but decided not to pawn it after all. She had enough now, more than enough, to pay for the girls' summer camp.

While she was proud of herself for how she got the pawnbroker to come up from $100 to $400, she wanted to kick herself for not first getting the vase appraised. Surely, if he gave her $400, it could have indeed been worth $1,000, perhaps even more. She was determined, even though she wouldn't be able to do it any time soon, to get that vase out of hock and see what its true value was.

While Lora was out, Cecilia and Veronica were at Mama J's. It was the weekend for her family's visit. Cecilia and Veronica were always invited to come over and play with her grandchildren and eat.

When Lora arrived at home, she unloaded the lawn equipment from the trunk of her Ford station wagon and put it in the shed on the side of her house. Although Mama J was expecting her to join her family and the girls, she decided to first take a shower and put on a summer dress and sandals. She wanted to look the way she felt, which was very good.

Lora was a relatively small woman—five-foot-three, 120 pounds. But by no means was she fragile or petite looking. She had high, squared shoulders and well-defined biceps and calves. The athleticism of her body was offset by the soft curvature of her bosom and hips that were accentuated by her tiny waist. She never knew who her father was, but her mother was biracial, and Lora appeared to be mixed (a "mutt" as Big Lucy would say), evidenced by her caramel complexion and soft, wavy, dark hair. What drew attention to Lora was her posture and gait. She always walked with an air of confidence—her head high, shoulders back and graceful yet long, deliberate steps.

◆ ◆ ◆

Every other Saturday morning for the next two months, the neighborhood would vibrate with the noise of the lawnmowers as Lora and the men in the neighborhood mowed their lawns. It was common practice in the neighborhood to mow on the same day so that the sprawling front lawns had a uniform appearance.

Since Lora had started mowing her lawn herself, the fumes from everyone's gas-powered lawnmowers were not the only thing fouling the air.

Perceptions

More disturbing was the attention Lora was getting from the men. Now they were taking an inordinate amount of breaks to sit, sip lemonade and rest—and what rested most were their eyes, on Lora. While her overalls and floppy hat concealed her physicality, the grace in which she moved revealed her attractiveness. Also what the men found attractive was a woman doing "a man's job." Even cranky Mr. Felix, whom no one had ever seen smile, had a smile on his face on mowing day.

This did not go unnoticed by the suspicious eyes of Big Lucy, the observing eyes of Edna and the discerning eyes of Mama J. So, after about two months, the ladies trooped together to Mama J's house to discuss the matter.

"It's not like they are going out and having an affair or going to one of those nasty places where women strip their clothes off," Mama J said as she tried to placate the ladies.

"Well it's still lust and, Mama J, *you* should know better than anyone, because it's in the Bible—lust is sinful," Big Lucy said in a preachy tone.

"Well it's not so much my Walter looking at her. After all, she is attractive. What I don't like is his snippy little comments like asking me if I ever cut a lawn? Now that man has known me all my life and knows I have never cut a yard," declared Edna.

"One thing we all know, ladies, is that this is not Lora's fault. She has done nothing to encourage the men, and I'm quite sure she is unaware of the attention she is getting," Mama J advised. Both Edna and Big Lucy agreed.

"The only reason she cuts her own yard is because she doesn't have a man to do it for her and because, as she told me, she doesn't have the money to keep paying for a lawn service," Mama J further advised.

"Well, what we supposed to do? Put blindfolds on the men, or maybe pay for someone to cut her yard?" Big Lucy said sarcastically.

"You know, Lucy, you just gave me an idea," Mama J said earnestly.

"What?" asked Big Lucy and Edna.

"Edna, Danny is old enough to cut yards, and helps Walter cut yours all the time. Why don't we ask him to cut her yard at a price she can afford? And I'm sure he can use some extra money."

"Why, Mama J, that's a good idea!" Edna said, pleased with the idea, as was Big Lucy.

"Okay, Edna you talk to Danny to see if he is willing—"

"Oh he'll be willing" Edna interjected, assuring the ladies.

"And come Sunday, after church, I'll go talk to Lora," Mama J said.

"Question is, is she is going to cooperate?" asked Big Lucy.

"I'm as sure as my faith in Jesus," Mama J replied.

With that said, Edna and Big Lucy headed back to their houses to prepare dinner for their husbands.

Perceptions

Mama J headed to the vegetable garden in her backyard to water her collard greens, but something she said was perplexing her. The withering thirsty greens begging for water looked like the remorse she felt in her heart, begging for forgiveness—for saying that she was as sure as her faith in Jesus that Lora would cooperate. It bristled against her faith to suggest anything in her earthly world was as important as her relationship to Jesus. She prayed, "Dear Jesus, there is nothing, absolutely nothing, that I am more sure of than my faith in you. Please forgive me for saying what I said. But do realize we need Lora to cooperate."

The following day, when Danny came home from school, Edna told him about the plan but was not sure how much he would be paid. He was excited because for quite some time he had wanted to find a way to make some extra money instead of relying on the monthly allowance his parents gave him. But, more particularly, because Lora had no man to help her, and the girls had no father.

Danny was born to Edna and Walter when Edna was 40. While they had always wanted children, he was their first and only child. He also had been the only child to grow up in the neighborhood. Whether it was because of this environment or his nature, one might describe Danny as an old soul. He preferred jazz and rhythm and blues to pop music; he preferred movie classics to action flicks; he preferred a quiet day of fishing at a pond rather than hanging out at the mall playing arcade games. He was an honor student, good at sports and had looks that made him "eye candy" for the girls at school. Not only did he act older, but he looked older. At 15, he stood over six feet, and seemed taller because of his long legs. He was not buff, but rather he was lean with broad shoulders and a tapered waist. His dark complexion emphasized his perfect white teeth when he smiled. But what made him stand out and be admired by his classmates and adults the most was his mature demeanor and composure. When he spoke, he spoke gently—always careful to not speak too loud or harshly, even if he were vexed or angry. He always thought before speaking so as not to offend, and he always listened before responding. He was confident, but never cocky. He was taught by Walter and Edna, and their church, that men should protect women, and that children were God's greatest gift.

That Sunday, after church, Mama J paid Lora a visit, just as she promised the ladies. While her purpose was to talk with Lora about the lawn cutting, she had on her mind something more important to talk with Lora about. For this visit, she had not given Lora prior notice, feeling that they were acquainted well enough for her to pop call.

"Mama J, it's so good to see you! Come on in, have a seat. Can I get you something to drink?" Lora said surprised and happy to see her.

"A cold glass of water would be fine," Mama J replied as she took a seat in the Queen Anne chair.

"You look lovely. How was church?" Lora asked, as she returned with a tall glass of ice cold water in one of her better glasses.

"Good, good—as always. Where are the girls?" Mama J inquired, noticing that the house was so quiet.

"They're at a birthday party for one of their friends. Don't have to pick them up until 4:30," Lora replied as she looked at her watch, which now read a little after 2:30.

"Well can we talk a little bit now, before they get home?" Mama J asked with a slight quiver in her voice.

"Of course, you can talk with me anytime. But you look a little stressed. Is there anything wrong?" Lora asked, knowing that this demeanor was uncharacteristic of Mama J.

"No, I just have some things on my mind...some concerns about you."

"Me? Did I do something wrong?"

"No, no, and don't take my concerns as something you did wrong. Rather, they are things that maybe you should be doing, or things you might do in a better way. Do you follow me?"

"Yes, ma'am," Lora answered politely.

"Lora, how come you don't go to church? Not my church, just any church?"

"You are not the first person who has asked me this. I usually just tell people it's none of their business. But I don't mind telling you because I feel you care about me, and you feel like a mother to me."

"You are so right about me caring about you. Like you, I had to raise my children—all nine of them."

"Nine?" Lora was surprised that Mama J had that many children.

"Yep, weren't no birth control in my day like it is now. And no courts to make men pay child support. My husband ran off with a floozy. Kinda similar to your situation. Maybe not the floozy, but similar. Also, like you, I had no family to help me. But I joined the church and found the Lord. So why haven't you, Lora?"

"I have never lost the Lord—not really. I guess that's because I feel he is always with me, protecting me. But what I have lost is any belief in organized religions," Lora went on to explain.

"I loved my adoptive parents, and it truly hurt me when they disowned me because I no longer wanted to be a Jehovah's Witness. Because I wanted to know about other faiths, and questioned some of their practices, I was dis-fellowshipped by the congregation. At 18, they told me I could no longer live under their roof. For several years, I tried to make amends with them. But they said the only way I could be part of their life was to be a Jehovah's Witness.

Mama J thought Jehovah's Witnesses were fine people, but it disturbed her to know that they would disassociate themselves from their *own* children.

Lora continued. "I have had many friends of different religions—loving, good people—but they always felt their religion was the only one that was right—everyone else was wrong. I look at history and what's going on in this world now. Instead of religion uniting people, it has caused wars, divided people, family, cultures. That is why I don't go to church, or like to talk about religion."

"Oh, Jesus," Mama J uttered knowing that a refutation would take her hours, or a whole lot of Bible study classes.

"I want to show you something, Mama J." Lora went to her dining room and brought back a wooden box and a Bible. She opened the box and took out several items one by one, explaining to Mama J their significance.

"This is a *zhong gon*. It was given to me by Chin, my roommate in college who was a Buddhist. She hung it on the door of our dorm room. It is supposed to bring good fortune to your home. She gave it to me when we graduated.

"This is called a prayer mat that the Muslims use to kneel on as they pray. It was given to me by Qasim, a young man from Pakistan whose entire family was killed in a religious war.

"This is a book that I read in high school—*The Diary of Anne Frank*—a story about the Holocaust.

I'm sure you are familiar with what happened to the Jews.

"This is a photo of Rod, a friend of mine in high school, who killed himself because he was gay, and because his parents told him he was a sinner and that God did not love him.

"This is a book written in the early 1900s by William James—*Varieties of the Religious Experience.* He talks about man's need to believe in a higher being, and that it's because of personal experiences that there are so many different religions—and why people are so faithful to the religion they choose.

"And this is my Bible. While I do not attend church or have a religious affiliation, I do believe in its teachings and honor Jesus for the sacrifices he made for us."

Lora sat there waiting for Mama J's response, expecting a sermon like others would do, trying to convert her to their religion. But Mama J just sat there silently. Finally, Lora asked, "Aren't you going to say anything?"

"Nope. Come here, child, I just want to hold you." As Mama J held Lora, she prayed to Jesus to give Lora understanding—that to be faithful, she needed to go to church. Mama J also thought to herself that she would never forsake Lora like her adoptive parents did.

"Okay, now I want to talk to you about something else, and give you some motherly advice," Mama J said. "And I don't want you interrupting me until I'm finished. Just like I didn't interrupt you when you were explainin'," Mama J demanded as she gestured to Lora's keepsakes. Lora nodded her head obediently.

"I want you to stop cutting your own yard. You are a distraction in the neighborhood. All the men are looking at you and the women are getting uneasy. We know you have done nothing to encourage this. But men are men, and the dog comes out in them when it comes to certain things, one of them is when they see a pretty woman. I know that you are just trying to save money and can't afford to hire a lawn service, but I can get you someone who can cut the yard for probably half the cost, maybe less. Now you can talk."

Mama J leaned back, took a sip of the now lukewarm water, and waited for Lora's response.

Lora, surprised, befuddled and embarrassed, replied, "I had no idea, I'm so sorry—"

Mama J interjected, saying, "I already told you it's not your fault, so stop apologizing. Just need to know will you stop cutting your yard if I can get someone to cut it at a price you can afford? And what can you afford?"

"Well, of course I'll stop. You and the ladies' friendship means so much to me. Besides, it will give me more time to spend with the girls. How much can I afford? Um, half the cost would be $10. I can swing that."

"Good, that's all I need to know. I gotta go now. These shoes are killin' me. And it should be time for you to pick up the girls."

Lora and Mama J gave each other another hug and said good day.

Mama J's church shoes were beginning to make her feet swell like two little sausages plumping up on the fire. But she decided to endure a little longer and triumphantly headed to Edna's house to tell her the good news.

The following Saturday, at 9 o'clock sharp, Lora heard the sound of the lawnmowers being cranked up. She peeped through the blinds and saw Danny approaching her yard. She went out to meet him.

"So, *you* are my new yard man?" she said smiling as she reached out to shake his hand.

"At your service, ma'am," he replied as his large hand shook her small hand.

"Come with me, I'll show you where I keep everything. The lawnmower still has enough oil and gas from the last cut." As he was unloading the lawn equipment from the shed, Lora told him how much she appreciated his help, that it would give her more time to spend with her girls and that one of the things she wanted to do with them on Saturdays was teach them to play tennis.

Danny shared that he had always wanted to learn tennis, but his father preferred he learn basketball because of his wing span.

Lora asked, "What is a wing span?"

He held up both his arms and stretched them out side to side to demonstrate. "If you measure from the tip of your left-hand middle finger to the tip of your right-hand middle finger, that is your wing span."

"So what does yours measure?"

"Six feet, ten inches," he replied somewhat coyly so not to sound like he was bragging.

"Now I've learned something new—a 'wing span.' Well, let me not hold you up. Let me know if you need anything," she said as she headed back to the house and Danny cranked up the lawnmower.

The men in the neighborhood finished rather early that day. Perhaps this was because they had no distractions, so thought the ladies. Edna was proud of her boy as she watched him cut Lora's lawn; Mama J and Lucy were grateful; and the men were, some might describe, disenchanted.

When Danny was finished, he called Lora out to inspect his work. She said it was remarkable as she looked at how meticulously he had done the edging—superior to the job the professional service had done, and something she found difficult. He then put the lawn equipment back in the shed as she went inside to get his $10. She thanked him and then tip toed up to give him a hug. His dark complexion hid his blushing. Lora went back into her house to finish her laundry, as Danny headed back to his house. The butterflies that swarmed around as he was cutting Lora's yard felt like they were now in his stomach.

CHAPTER IV

The Call

THE HOT SUMMER AND GAIETY OF CHILDREN being out of school and playing outdoors gave way to the breezy fall and children back in school, as evidenced by the yellow school buses that made their way throughout neighborhoods. This would be the first year that Cecilia and Veronica, who were now seven, would be taking the morning school bus. Lora felt they were old enough, and it was good that they learn a sense of independence. Lora's concern for how they would adjust to this new arrangement was relieved the first day.

"I got to be the line leader," bragged Cecelia.

"Yes, and everyone wanted to sit next to me," said Veronica.

"No, just two people," argued Cecelia.

Because Lora had to work until 4:00 pm and the girls got out of school at 2:30, they were enrolled in an after-school program. Complaints had been made that the program was run like a detention center where children just sat watching the clock go *tick tock* until their parents arrived. However, because of Lora's and other parents' complaints, it was brought to the attention of the school officials, and changes were made. Now the children were engaged in after school activities that included arts and crafts, intramural sports and games, and staff that helped children with homework.

There was harmony in the neighborhood with Danny cutting Lora's yard, and it gave her the opportunity to take the girls to the playground and teach them tennis. While she was far from a pro, she had enough skills to teach the girls.

With the fading summer, lawns did not need to be cut as frequently, but the falling autumn leaves were just as demanding. Every Saturday Danny would rake up the leaves that were abundant in Lora's yard because of her two oak trees. He would rake them into a big pile. Often times, before he could pack the leaves into garbage bags, Cecilia and Veronica would come home from tennis practice and jump on the pile—like it was a trampoline—scattering the leaves everywhere. This irritated Lora, for which she made them pick up the scattered leaves and put them back on the pile. Danny thought the girls' jumping on their imaginary trampoline was hilarious—something he wanted to do at their age when Walter raked up the leaves. He also felt that it was his fault because he had not bagged everything up, which he confessed to Lora. To placate Lora and so that the girls could still enjoy their leaf trampoline, he told Lora it was good that the girls jumped on the leaves; that it made the leaves more pliable, thus easier to bag. "Was this true?" Danny thought. "Yeah, when you think about it."

◆ ◆ ◆

While everyone enjoyed the beauty of the changing seasons, and they did not have to endure harsh winters, this winter seemed a bit different. It was unusually cold, dark and drizzly with high occurrences of thunderstorms. In spite of the dreary weather, after Thanksgiving, Christmas lights were hung and all the neighbors decorated their yards with a theme to celebrate the holiday season.

Lora was particularly excited because it would be her first Christmas in her new home. The nursery was closed for the holidays, and she did not have to go to work until after New Year. Mama J was always excited about Christmas Day because it was the day her beloved Jesus was born. For Big Lucy and Milky, it was a day that they spent at the homeless center bringing and serving food. For Edna and Walter, it was extra joyful because Danny was born on Christmas Day.

Danny had saved up all the money he received from cutting and raking up the leaves in Lora's yard to buy a special gift for Cecilia and Veronica—a trampoline. However, he did not have quite enough so he asked his parents if he could have in advance the $100 they usually gave him for his birthday. Walter said yes without hesitation and asked no questions. Edna, however, insisted on knowing why.

"Because I always wanted a trampoline when I was younger, but never asked you. Besides, I had no one I could enjoy it with. It'll be fun for them, and for Mama J's grandchildren when they come over," he said as persuasively as he could. "And you might want to even try a few jumps yourself," he teasingly added.

Edna pointed her finger at him and replied, "Boy, you had me until you said about me jumping on that thing. But alright. I'll give it to you on Friday, and if you want, you can go with me to Kmart and the mall on Friday. There are going to be a lot of sales, and I need to do some Christmas shopping as well."

So they went to Kmart and the mall that Friday. As Edna did her shopping, Danny did his. He found a trampoline that he thought the girls would like. He asked the sales person about its safety and warranty. He was assured that it was top of the line. Its cost left him with $50. He bought his mother a set of Christmas-themed kitchen towels and a set of glasses to replace the many that he had clumsily broken. He kept up tradition by buying Walter a tie—something he bought every Christmas for his father, who proudly wore it to church the following Sunday. Now Danny had $20 left and went to look for something he badly wanted for himself.

The Call

He found it for only $15—a tennis racket. But then he changed his mind. There was another present that was more important than the tennis racket. He looked throughout the mall and finally found a store that had it.

"I need it engraved. How much will that cost?" Fifty cents per letter, he was told. He dug in his pockets and took out all his loose change, but still he did not have enough. "I only have enough for four letters, so just make it L-O-R-A." He did not have enough for *MRS. JONES*.

Christmas Day came and the weather had improved. It was warm for a winter day, and the skies were clear. That morning the girls, in glee and excitement, opened the presents Lora had bought them. Lora received handmade gifts from the girls, and like a typical mother reacted to them as if they were diamonds. That afternoon, the girls put on their Santa caps and went with their mother to deliver jars of homemade strawberry jam that they made for the neighbors, including cranky Mr. Felix. He was not home, but they left it on his doorstep. Lora bought two special gifts and cards. One was for Mama J—a pair of Isotoner slippers that were supposed to be the most comfortable slippers on the market. On the card she wrote, *You are a blessing from God. Thank you for all that you do for me and the girls, Love, Lora.* She had the girls sign their names as well. The other present was for Danny—a tennis racket and a card on which she wrote, *To a very special young man. Hope someday you'll learn to play tennis,* signed by her and the girls.

To keep the trampoline a surprise, while Lora and the girls were delivering the jars of jam, Danny and Walter went into Lora's backyard and assembled it quickly. Mama J, covertly, kept Lora and the girls at her house until Edna signaled that the coast was clear. It was the highlight of the day as Mama J's grandchildren came over and joined the girls, screaming with delight and jumping on the trampoline. All the adults soon retreated back into their houses to get Christmas dinner ready. Danny, however, stayed with the kids to make sure no one got hurt on the trampoline, and also because he was having as much fun as the kids.

Lora started to get dinner ready, knowing that the girls would be exhausted and hungry after all the jumping, which she estimated would be in an hour. She had cooked the night before, so all she had to do was heat things up and pop the dinner rolls in the oven. She set the dining room table with the snowman face plates and matching glasses that she bought for the girls. In the center of the table she placed one of the gifts that the girls had made for her—a nativity scene made of colored construction paper, and a little baby Jesus made of Play-Doh and wrapped in a blanket made of gauze. It had been a school project that the girls had worked on. They hid it in their closet to give to Lora for Christmas. But she found it before Christmas because she frequently checked their room. She did not tell the girls she had found it, but she did make a mental note to find a special place for it on Christmas Day.

Just as Lora's motherly instinct told her, the girls came bursting through the door an hour later, shouting "I'm so tired! I'm so hungry!" Danny was right behind them, but he did not look tired at all. Lora had just come out of their bathroom where she had filled the bathtub for them. They were still at the age where they enjoyed taking baths together.

"And you're so sweaty too," Lora shouted back to them. "Get in the bathroom and take a bath. And then put on your new Christmas PJs. When you're done, dinner will be ready." Without hesitation, the girls headed to the bathroom, excited about wearing their new pajamas, and hungry for the turkey that they could smell as it was heating up in the oven.

As the girls scurried to the bathroom, Lora and Danny just stood there looking at one another — that kind of look where words cannot express the way you feel, but the other knows intuitively — the happiness that Lora and Danny felt about the day.

"They really love that trampoline, Danny."

"Yes, but I do want to caution you, Mrs. Jones. They need to be watched until they learn to jump better. I have heard of accidents."

"I'll be sure to do that. Thanks for letting me know. Oh yes, the girls and I also bought you a present." Lora went over and got the tennis racket from under the tree. It was wrapped in a box covered in red and silver paper and tied with a handmade white bow. She handed it to him with the card.

Danny concealed his surprise and emotions. "Should I open it now?"

"Why not?" Lora asked.

"Because your food smells like it's burning."

"Oh my goodness, oh my goodness!" Lora yelled as she ran to the kitchen. Indeed, the turkey was burned—but still salvageable, she hoped—as she scraped off the burnt part and cut out parts that were still moist. She tasted a piece. "Well it might not look like a turkey anymore, but it still tastes like one," she said to herself with relief.

Remembering Danny, she headed back to the living room, but he was already gone. She glanced over at the tree to see if the tennis racket was still there. It was not. Instead there was a small package wrapped in forest green paper and tied with a bamboo string, with a sticker that read *To Mrs. Jones, From Danny.* She immediately wanted to open it, but decided to wait until later as the girls pranced out in their new pajamas and yelled, "Mommy, we're ready for dinner!"

After dinner and the girls retired, Lora sat in her bed with the nightstand lamp on. She reached over to get the present that Danny had given her. Before dinner, she had put it on her nightstand to make sure the girls did not open it. She untied the bamboo string and removed the wrapping paper.

It was a brown leather-bound journal with her name engraved on the front—*LORA*. She thumbed through the blank pages imagining the many things she wanted to write about. As she put the journal back on the nightstand and turned off the light, she thought once again "How could someone so young be so kind and thoughtful?"

◆ ◆ ◆

Edna went to clean up her kitchen and took out containers to put away the leftovers. But there were barely any—just one sliver of ham, and the turkey carcass which maybe had just enough meat to make a soup. There was absolutely no macaroni and cheese left—the pan was so clean it didn't even look like it needed to be washed. She was irritated that Walter had used one of the Christmas towels that Danny had given her—they were to be used just for show.

"Walter, you coming to bed?" she yelled as she left the kitchen. "Danny, make sure you turn off those Christmas lights, unless you want to pay the light bill. And I will make you pay it, now that I know you got enough money to buy a trampoline," she yelled and then chuckled.

Danny was in his room putting up the presents his parents had given him—clothes, a pair of sneakers, and from his father, a poster of Magic Johnson for his wall. He picked up his present from Lora. He looked at how nicely it was wrapped and thought it was a shame that something so nice looking had to be destroyed by opening it. While he meticulously tried to untie the bow, hoping it could be re-used, his large hands would not let him and it came completely apart. With that, he tore open the box. "Mrs. Jones, Mrs. Jones, how did you know?" he quietly exclaimed. He jumped up and started swinging the racket, and then fell on his back on his bed smiling, until it dawned on him he had better turn off the Christmas lights.

As all the neighbors turned off their Christmas lights that night, nature turned on its own lights with the beauty of twinkling stars and the sound of silence. The neighborhood went to sleep—some people feeling exhausted, some feeling content, some feeling blessed, some feeling that they could hardly wait until tomorrow.

◆ ◆ ◆

"Mommy, Mommy, wake up," Cecilia and Veronica begged as they tugged on Lora's shoulders.

"Noooo, Mommy does not want to get up now," Lora pleaded.

"But Mr. Sunshine is up and waiting for you," Veronica said as both girls gave each other a wink.

Lora reluctantly woke up and sat up in bed. "What's going on?" she asked, annoyed.

The Call

"Can we go outside and play on the trampoline?" Cecilia asked.

"No! Get your little tails back to your room right now! Do you realize it's only…" Lora looked at the alarm clock and realized it was later than she thought. "I'll be up soon. Now get out of here." As the two little feeling rejected girls turned around with their heads bowed to go back to their room, Lora muttered, "Just give Mommy 10 more minutes to sleep, then I'll get up, fix you breakfast, and we'll all go outside and play on the trampoline." Cecilia and Veronica looked at each other and silently clapped their hands saying "Yay!" as they tip toed back to their room.

Despite the big dinner they ate the evening before, Lora was famished that morning and decided to cook a big breakfast—grits, sausage, scrambled eggs with cheese and pancakes. The girls joined her in the kitchen to help with the pancakes. They were not interested in anything else—just give them pancakes and they were fine. When they finished eating, Lora realized that her eyes had been bigger than her stomach as she moaned and looked at the leftover food on her plate. The girls noticed too and looked at her as if to say "Poor Mommy," sympathizing with her over-stuffed stomach, and knowing that Mommy did not like to waste food.

"Too bad we don't have a dog. It would love this," she said as she looked at the leftovers on her plate. And then she immediately thought, "Why did I just say that?" Simultaneously and instantly, the girls' heads jerked up as they turned and looked at each other, turned back and looked at Lora. With eyes as big as saucers, they pleaded, "Can we, Mommy, please, please, can we have a dog?"

"No!" Lora said with authority and gave them that look that said "Case closed!"

After breakfast the girls and Lora got dressed in jeans, winter sweaters and boots, and headed out to the trampoline for a morning of fun. After about two hours Lora had had enough, while the girls were still going like they just got started. However, remembering what Danny said, she told them they could not play on the trampoline without supervision. They were disappointed, but only momentarily as they remembered the other toys that they got for Christmas and had yet to play with, and hurried inside to their room. Lora kicked off her boots at the door, went to her room, and decided she needed a shower after all that jumping.

As she dressed after her shower, the phone on her nightstand rang.

"Hello... Yes, this is Mrs. Jones."

"What? Yes...yes...yes...."

Her hands started to tremble and her legs shook.

"But how? ... When? ... Why? ... Where?"

"Hold on, I need to get something to write with."

Lora found a pen in the drawer of the nightstand, among the medications she kept in case she or the girls got sick.

The Call

She couldn't find any paper, but then she saw the journal that Danny gave her, grabbed it and opened it to its first page.

"Okay, where?" She wrote hastily as she repeated what she heard: *New York Mount Sinai Hospital, Intensive Care Unit, Room 223.*

"Yes, yes, I am on my way. Thank you."

"Hello, hello, hello!" She wanted the telephone number, but the call had already disconnected.

She called Mama J. "Mama J, come quickly, I need you! Please, please, I need you!"

Mama put on her house slippers and hurried over. She didn't bother ringing the doorbell as she opened the unlocked door. Lora heard her come in and called out, "I'm in my bedroom." Lora sat there, still trembling and shaking.

Mama J sat on the bed next to her. "What in the world is going on?" she asked worriedly, trying to hold Lora's trembling hand.

"It's my husband, he's hurt, he's in the hospital! They said he's dying!"

Lora gave her the details of the telephone call. A lady who identified herself as a nurse said she was calling from Mount Sinai Hospital in New York City; that Lora was listed on the contact information of patient Joseph J. Jones; that Mr. Jones was in the intensive care unit and not expected to live much longer; that because of confidentiality they could not release any further information; that the patient is presently under medication and care that would not allow him to speak directly to her; that if Lora would like, she could visit the patient, but it should be as soon as possible.

"Mama J, I have to get to New York!" Lora tearfully exclaimed.

Mama J stood up and took both of Lora's hands. "Okay, but first I want you to compose yourself. Your shaking and trembling ain't gonna do you no good. I want you to stay in this room until you do. In the meantime, I am going to shut your door, and let me take care of things."

Mama J looked at the phone. "You got another phone in the house?"

"Yes, in the kitchen," Lora replied.

"Okay, like I said you just stay in here and compose yourself. Where are the girls?" Mama J asked.

"In their room," Lora replied as she tried to compose herself.

"Well they don't need to see you like this. Do you understand, Lora?" Mama J firmly asked.

"Yes, Mama J," Lora replied meekly.

As Mama J left Lora and was about to close the door, she thought to tell Lora she needed to pray. But she decided not to, feeling that Lora already knew this. She then went to the girls' room and told them to be good little girls, and to stay in their room while she helps Mommy with some things. She then went to the kitchen and picked up the phone.

The Call

"Hello, Edna, I need you to drop whatever you're doing and get over to Lora's. It's an emergency. I'll explain when you get here. Just come on in, the door is unlocked."

"Hello, Milky, I need to speak with Lucy…no, it cannot wait, just hand her the phone through the door, I can't see her on the toilet…yes, it's that urgent…Lucy I need you to get over to Lora's as soon as you get off the toilet. I'll explain when you get here. The door is unlocked, so just come in."

Edna arrived just as Mama J hung up; Big Lucy, a few minutes later. Mama J took them to the dining room, away from earshot of the girls. She let them know that Lora was in her bedroom. She re-capped the telephone call Lora received from the hospital.

"Lora needs to get to New York today, and she needs our help." Both Edna and Lucy agreed and asked what needed to be done.

"Big Lucy, I want you to call the airlines and see what flights are available. Because of the holidays, all flights might be booked. In that case, call Amtrak and Greyhound. See which one has the quickest time to New York. Book whatever will get Lora to New York the quickest and find out the cost. Best that you go home and get Milky to help you, since he works at the airport."

Big Lucy hurried out the door to enlist Milky's help.

"Edna, I want you to take the girls over to your house and have Danny watch them. Tell Walter we are going to need him to drive Lora to the airport, train station, Greyhound, whatever the case may be. When you're done, get back over here and help Lora pack."

Edna went to the girls' bedroom. "Danny wants you to come over. He has some card tricks he wants to show you," she said trying to entice the girls.

Mama J went back into the Lora's bedroom. "Lora, how much cash do you have on hand?"

Lora started riffling around, looking in her purse, the stash money she has hidden in her bedroom, and considered the jar of loose change in the kitchen. "$150 not counting about $20 of change in the kitchen. But I do have about $300 in the bank."

"Bank ain't going to help. They all closed for the next two days because of Christmas. Don't worry, I'll figure it out. I want you to start packing. Remember it's freezing now in New York. Still, pack as light as possible. You don't want to have to lug around a lot of suitcases."

Lora went to her closet, looking for a suitcase.

"I'll be right back. If Edna and Big Lucy get back before I do, tell them to wait," Mama J said as she headed out of the house.

"But Mama J, who is going to take care of the girls?" Lora shouted.

"Me! Their godmother!" Mama J shouted back as she headed back to her house.

Edna returned first and let Lora know that the girls were safe and sound. She proceeded to help

The Call

Lora pack things into the small suitcase that was bulging from the winter wear. Lora sat on it as she tried to zip it up. "Child, move, my big butt can do that," Edna said as she sat on the suitcase and easily zipped it up.

Mama J returned. "Girls situated?" she asked, to which Edna said yes. "Lora, if is okay with you, the girls will be staying at my house while you're gone, and I am sure Edna and Big Lucy will help if I need anything. Is there any special things we need to know, like what they like to eat, what time they should go to bed?"

"No, not really. Whatever you think is best. Just make sure you tell them Mommy has to take care of some important things and that I'll call them every day, and that I'll be back as soon—"

Lora was interrupted as Big Lucy burst through the door. "Great news, everyone! Milky used his connections to get Lora on a flight out of Augusta Regional at 4:30. Arrives in New York at 6:30. However, it's only one way and kinda expensive—$250."

"But I only have—" Lora started to say as she was interrupted by Mama J.

"Great job, Lucy, and God bless Milky." Mama J looked on the clock on Lora's living room wall. "It's 2:15 now. Edna, tell Walter that Lora needs to leave in a half an hour. The lines might be long with so many traveling for the holidays."

Big Lucy said, "It might be good if Milky goes with Walter. Him being a skycap, he can get Lora's ticket and baggage checked quicker."

Mama J instructed Edna and Big Lucy to go tell the men the plans while she and Lora packed some things for the girls' stay at her house.

When Edna and Big Lucy left, Mama J reached into the pocket of her house dress and handed Lora some rolled up bills. "Here is $500. This with your $150 should cover the plane fair, taxicabs and a hotel for a couple of days. You say you have some money in the bank. Banks should be open in two days. If you run short, I can wire some more money to you. Call me collect. I need to know that you are okay, and the girls need to hear from you."

Lora started tearing up, expressing her gratitude, but Mama J abruptly cut her off. "Now is not the time for sentiments or tears. Right now you need to be strong for your sake and the girls, and no tellin' what you're going to have to go through when you get to the hospital. Now get dressed for the airport, and make sure to take your identification, and don't forget to pack your toothbrush. I'm going to make sure everything is locked up while you're gone. I'll keep the keys and I'll need to come back over here for more of the girls' stuff. When you go over to say goodbye to the girls, remember what I said about being strong. Don't let them see you cry," Mama J commanded.

It was now 2:45 and Walter and Milky were sitting in the car waiting for Lora as she went to say goodbye to the girls.

"Mommy, Mommy," they shouted. "Danny taught us a card trick. Come, we'll show you!" Then they noticed how Lora was dressed and looked puzzled. "Why are you wearing that coat?" asked Cecilia. "And boots?" asked Veronica.

"Mommy is going on a short trip to New York because she has some important things to take care of. While I am gone, you are going to be taken well care of by Mama J, Ms. Edna and Ms. Lucy."

"No, we want to go with you," Cecilia sulked.

"It's too cold up there, and besides there is nothing fun up there to do," Lora tried to convince them.

"But we want to go," Cecilia pleaded while Veronica whimpered.

"No buts or whining, young ladies. Mommy has to do what she has to do, and while I'm gone I expect you to do what you have to do—be on your best behavior and do what Mama J, Ms. Edna and Ms. Lucy tell you. Case closed. Now give me a kiss and a hug. I have to go," she commanded.

The girls reluctantly complied with no more refutes, and affectionately gave their mother a kiss and hug. "Bye, Mommy," they gently said as Lora headed out to the car.

At the last minute, Danny pleaded with Edna if he could go along for the ride, to which she consented. Milky sat in the front with Walter, Danny in the back with Lora. The ladies waved goodbye as Lora, and the men and Danny headed to the airport. Unlike the ladies, the men refrained from talking. It was a time for silence. And in the silence, Lora reached over and held tightly to Danny's hand until they got to the airport.

◆ ◆ ◆

Lora was in a window seat. The fully booked plane was relatively quiet except for the sounds of a crying baby in the back of the plane. She felt somewhat guilty by not feeling more apprehension about leaving the girls—she had never been apart from them. But she could not worry about the girls. She was too consumed with worry about what had happened to her husband.

What has happened to Joseph?

She leaned back in her seat, rested the side of her head against the window, closed her eyes and for the duration of the two-hour flight, reminisced about her life with Joseph—how they met, how they fell in love, how happy she was when they were married, when the girls were born.

CHAPTER V

Joseph

IN 1972, AFTER LORA RECEIVED HER ASSOCIATE OF Arts degree in horticulture from San Jose State University, she headed to New York. What was attractive to her about the city was its diverse culture, with neighborhoods embracing their own culture while proud to be New Yorkers. She found it ironic that while she was surrounded by so many people on the busy sideways and subway, she still felt alone—as if she were invisible. She felt that even if she walked naked through the crowds of people, no one would notice her. Because she was an introvert, she liked this feeling. While she liked being alone, however, there were times when she did feel lonely.

That Monday, after work at the flower shop, she took the D train to her Brooklyn neighborhood. She stopped at the local grocery store and then walked to her apartment building two blocks away. She put her two bags on the front store stoop as she fumbled for keys in her purse. But before she could find her keys, one of the tenants opened the door and held it open for her. As he saw her grocery bags, he offered to carry them to her apartment. He understood her hesitation and assured her it was okay—he lived on the third floor, apartment 3D. His persuasiveness, her tired feet and the heavy bags—filled with mostly canned goods—gave way to her caution, and she accepted his offer.

"What floor, Miss Lady?" he asked.

"Fourth, apartment 4C," she replied as he headed up the stairs and she behind him.

"You like to cook? he asked as they ascended the stairs.

"Not really, but I like to eat," she replied.

"Well, cooking is me specialty," he said confidently, his Jamaican accent pronounced.

"Really?"

"Yeah mon, me a chef. Make da best curry goat, jerk chicken, salt fish, ackee, pigeon peas and rice, plantains in all Brooklyn," he said with pride. "Do you like Jamaican food?"

"I'm not a connoisseur, but I would say so," she replied.

"Well, why don't I make dinner for da pretty lady someday?" he asked as they reached the fourth floor where he placed the bags next to her door.

"Perhaps. Thank you for your help, Mister..."

"Jones, Joseph J. Jones," he said, reaching out to shake her hand. "And to whom do I have da pleasure?"

"Lora, Lora Jones," she replied, accepting his handshake.

"Ah, what a coincidence, we both Jones! See, we already have something in common, and da more reason why you should accept me dinner invitation."

"We'll see," she said smiling.

They bid each other a good evening, as he briskly walked down the stairs and Lora opened the door to her apartment.

The rest of the week and that weekend, she came home to containers of Jamaican food sitting in front of her door. Because he worked in the evenings at the restaurant, she rarely saw him. So she wrote him a note thanking him and letting him know how good the food was, and slipped it under his door. The restaurant where he worked was closed on Mondays, so he went up to her apartment that following Monday evening to deliver the food to her.

"Special order here for pretty lady," he called as he rang her doorbell.

She immediately recognized his voice, and opened the door. The food was piping hot and smelled delicious. "Oh, you are just completely spoiling me," she said as he handed her the food.

"Me don't spoil, me pamper. Pretty things should be pampered."

"Well, why don't you come in and join me?"

"No, me just delivery boy."

"No, seriously, you must come in and join me. Good food needs good company."

"Well said, pretty lady. I accept your most generous invitation."

He was awed by the way Lora had decorated her apartment, and he told her so. "Me feel like me in a Fifth Avenue apartment!" Unlike his apartment, hers was light and airy. The juxtaposition of the furniture made the apartment look roomy and comfortable. The pale grayish-blue walls gave a sense of serenity, while an eclectic assortment of figurines and framed posters popped the apartment with color and character. The orchids that hung in baskets from two corners in the ceilings aromatized the air.

They ate, talked and laughed until late in the night. While he had an undeniable Jamaican accent and used some patois expressions, she understood every word.

"So what does the J stand for, Joseph J. Jones?" Lora asked.

"John. But me got seven middle names," he answered.

"How's that?" Lora asked.

He swallowed his last bit of the curry chicken, knowing his answer was going to be a mouthful. "Me mom, who now rests in peace, was a devout Christian. She had said she wanted to name all her boys after names in the Bible starting with J. But I was to be her only boy, her only child, so she named me Joseph, John, Jeremiah, Joshua, Jonah, Job, Joel, Jude Jones."

"You have to be kidding!" Lora exclaimed trying to conceal her laughter causing her to almost choke on her plantain.

"Nope," he continued. "I ask her why she not give me da most important name—Jesus. She say da name Jesus sacred. I say Spanish people named Jesus. She say, no, they named Hey Sus. Me mom, not an educated woman, didn't realize Spanish people say J as H." They both laughed heartily.

"I figure, if I ever get married to a pretty lady like you, we will have plenty of names to name our sons after me, Jones Juniors," he teased.

"Suppose we have girls?" she teased back.

"Well, what is your middle name?" he asked.

"I don't have a middle name."

"Well then their names would be Precious, Pretty, Lovely, Beautiful, Gorgeous, Sweet, Charming...."

Lora burst out laughing again. He chuckled as well.

For the next several months they dated and grew to be an exclusive couple. He introduced her to his friends as *My Lady*. He changed to the day shift at the restaurant so that they could spend more time together. While she was an introvert, he took her to frequent Jamaican house parties and taught her to dance to reggae music. He took her to Rockefeller Center and taught her to ice skate, and he taught her how to play chess. Their weekend evenings included movies playing at the cinema near Times Square. Joseph wished he could afford to take her to a Broadway show, but Lora was content with a movie and afterwards a walk in Central Park, holding hands as lovers do.

There were other things about Joseph that made Lora admire and fall in love with him. While Joseph spoke in patois, he also could speak perfect English free from any Jamaican accent. He usually spoke this way when handling business matters or with people he did not know or he did not trust. Joseph was also fairly well educated, with a liberal arts degree from Brooklyn College. But his passion was always to be a chef.

On the weekend of Joseph's 26th birthday, Lora surprised him by re-decorating his apartment and throwing him a surprise birthday party. She arranged with his friend, Donald, to get him out of his apartment early that morning and not to let him come back until that night. She got a couple other close friends of his to come over and paint. The rest of his male friends, along with their wives and girlfriends, were invited to join in his birthday surprise party. They insisted on bringing the food and beverages.

During the week prior, she had shopped for a sofa slipcover to go over his worn corduroy sofa, decorative throw pillows and an accent rug to go under the coffee table. She bought matching drapes for the two windows that only had shades, and hung two baskets of ivy from the ceiling above each window. She bought two large posters and had them framed—one was a scenic poster of Dunn's River Falls, a place in Jamaica that he always talked about. The other was a print of Bob Marley, his favorite musician. She made sure to inform the apartment manager and fellow tenants about their party and said that she would turn down the music promptly at midnight. Most of the neighbors were of West Indian descent and said it was no problem, and wished her a merry time.

While Joseph was not completely surprised by the birthday party and his friends being there, he was completely surprised and overwhelmed by the transformation of his apartment. That night (rather early morning) as Lora and Joseph lay in bed, Joseph confided in her that he never had a birthday party, not even as a kid, and never had a place that looked so lovely. "Thank you, my pretty lady," he said as he kissed and held her passionately.

A month later, on her 23rd birthday, Joseph asked Lora to marry him. They got married at New York City Hall, and went to Jamaica to spend their honeymoon—climbing Dunn's River Falls, lying on the white sandy beach and making love in the warm, blue ocean.

During her pregnancy, Joseph waited on Lora hand and foot, and made sure she ate the best and healthiest of foods. At the doctor's appointments, he asked more questions than she could even think of—wanting to be assured that the baby was healthy. In her sixth month, the doctor said he wanted to do an ultrasound—a procedure that was not commonly done in the 1970s. The doctor said that Lora was unusually large for being six months, and he wanted to check for any abnormalities. Joseph was in the room when the ultrasound was being performed. As the doctor scanned Lora's belly and looked at the ultrasound monitor, Joseph was asking him, what does he see? The doctor finally answered that he saw two heads. Joseph screamed out, "Oh no! Me baby has two heads!" The doctor quickly relieved Joseph by telling him and Lora that they were having twins. Joseph left the doctor's office walking on air.

◆ ◆ ◆

"Ladies and gentlemen, we are preparing for landing. Please fasten your seat belts."

While Lora was waiting for her suitcase to come through the conveyor belt, she called Mama J collect and let her know that she had arrived safely and that now she was on the way to the hospital. Mama J informed her that the girls were at Edna's having dinner. Lora advised Mama J that because it would probably be late before she got out of the hospital, she would call tomorrow and let her know what was going on. "Give the girls a kiss for me, and tell them I love them... Yes, I will be strong... I love you too."

"Mount Sinai Hospital, please," she instructed the taxicab driver. He informed her it was a flat rate of $20. She was relieved because she wouldn't have to watch and hear the clicking meter, and also because it was less than she expected.

She entered the intimidating sky-reaching brown concrete building. She followed the arrows that led her to the elevator. She entered the elevator and pushed the button for the sixth floor. No one was in the elevator with her, and, as the door closed, she felt entrapped. The door opened at the sixth floor. She stood there, momentarily frozen. But the door refused to close, as if commanding her to depart. She finally exited the elevator and followed the arrows to the intensive care unit. Her legs felt like cement as she walked with fear and apprehension down the long corridor toward the nurses' station.

Her throat was dry as she tried to speak. "Hello, I am Lora Jones," she said to the woman at the desk. "I am here to see my husband, patient Joseph J. Jones, Room 223."

The attendant looked at the patient roster and asked Lora to please have a seat in one of the chairs that were lined up against the corridor wall. After about five minutes, a nurse approached Lora with a folder stamped in large red capital letters *Confidential*. On the second line in black letters it read

Patient Information. On the tab of the folder was a label which read *Joseph J. Jones.*

"Hello, I am Nurse Richards. I am the one that called you earlier," the soft spoken lady in white said as she took a seat on the chair next to Lora. "I am sorry I could not give you more information at that time. But after speaking with you, I spoke with Mr. Jones and told him that you were on your way to see him. He was very, very happy to hear this, and he gave us permission to release his patient information to you."

"Well, can I see him now?" Lora said anxiously.

Nurse Richards gently put her hand on Lora's shoulder and explained, "Yes, but because of the nature of his illness, the doctor needs to talk with you first."

"Illness?" Lora asked baffled. "I assumed he had been in an accident, a car accident. Did he have a heart attack, does he have cancer—"

Nurse Richards interrupted gently. "As I said, the doctor needs to talk with you. Please try to stay calm," she said, trying to sooth Lora. "The doctor is finishing up with a patient and should be out soon. Can I get you a cup of—" Before she could finish, she saw the doctor coming up to the nurses' station. "I see him now. Hold on, let me get him."

Lora watched as Nurse Richards went up the nurses' station, got the doctor's attention and handed him the folder, which he opened. He looked toward Lora and headed her way. "Hello,

Mrs. Jones, I am Dr. Goldstein," he said, extending his hand to shake hers. "Why don't you come with me where we can talk more privately." Lora followed him to a room with an executive mahogany desk and chair and two tapestry upholstered chairs. He sat in the executive desk chair and motioned for Lora to take a seat. Lora sat on the edge of one of the tapestry chairs with her knees tightly closed and holding her hands together even more tightly on her lap.

"Mrs. Jones, your husband has a disease called Acute Immune Deficiency Syndrome, also known as AIDS. There is no cure for this disease. Your husband is in the last stages and is not expected to live much longer."

The doctor waited for Lora's response and questions. He seemed surprised yet relieved, by her calmness.

"How much is not much longer, Doctor?" Lora asked.

"Any day. I am surprised that he is still alive. But I have seen patients linger for weeks, even months. Often times this is because of their will to live."

"How did he get this AIDS, Doctor?"

"That is the mystery of this disease. It is a virus that has recently surfaced. What we have discovered is that it is transmitted through blood and semen. We have also discovered that most of the patients have been either gay males, hemophiliacs, or drug addicts who share needles. From what we understand, your husband does not fit any of these profiles, so he could have contracted AIDS from a blood transfusion, giving blood at a blood bank or even from a dentist who did not use new or sterilized needles."

"I want to see my husband now," Lora said in a tone that suggested she was angry at the doctor. But the doctor was understanding. It was a reaction he commonly received when he had to deliver news that people did not want to hear or believe — he knew the meaning of the metaphoric phrase *shooting the messenger* quite well from his 30 years of practice.

"Before you do, I must tell you something else that is very important, and which the Centers for Disease Control has mandated we inform patients and their loved ones, since this is a contagious disease. Any person who has had sexual contact within seven years from the time a person is diagnosed with AIDS should be tested to see if they are infected.

"Yes, Doctor, thank you. Now I want to see my husband," she again insisted.

Dr. Goldstein escorted Lora back to the nurses' station and instructed the attendant to arrange for Lora to visit her husband. He shook her hand, gave her his condolences and told her to contact him or his staff if she had any questions. He also instructed the attendant to give Lora contact information for locations where she could go to be tested for AIDS.

JOSEPH

The attendant informed Lora that Nurse Richards was in the room with her husband now, and would be out shortly to get her. Lora asked where the bathroom was, and the attendant instructed her it was down the hall, two doors to her left. Lora proceeded to the bathroom, relieved herself and washed her hands. She then refreshed her lipstick and gave her hair a light brushing. She then took out her small vial of Chanel No. 5 perfume and gave a quick squirt to each side of her neck. When she returned to the nurses' station, Nurse Richards was there and she escorted her to Room 223.

"He is waiting to see you. I'll be out here if you need me," she said with a smile and misty eyes, knowing that Lora would be shocked by his appearance. Even though Nurse Richards had seen this so many times with patients' loved ones, she was still sensitive and sympathetic to their emotional pain.

Lora pushed open the door and entered the softly lit room. Joseph was seated in the bed, propped up with pillows. He was not hooked up to a lot of machines, an oxygen tank or heart monitor as Lora expected. Instead, what she saw was much worse than she could have ever imagined. Before her was a skeleton of the man she once knew. The strong, muscular body she remembered had shrunk down to fewer than 100 pounds. His radiant and smooth golden brown complexion was now ashy gray, and spotted with thick, round, dark soars. His full head of black, shiny, thick hair was now sparse and dull. Most sad was his face—his hollow cheeks and sunken, sad eyes.

"Hello, my pretty lady, I am so glad to see you," he said softly while lifting and opening his arms toward her. Hearing his voice erased all that was disturbing her heart. She dropped her purse and ran to his embrace. As they held each other, she cried harder than she had ever known possible—not because of his condition, but because she was so happy to see him.

The love she still had for him could not be denied.

As they finally broke their embrace, Lora sat on the chair next to his bed and held his fragile hand with one hand, and with the other wiped the tears from her eyes with tissues from the box that sat on the nightstand next to Joseph's bed.

"Me nurse tells me that you spoke with the doctor. So you understand my condition, Lora?"

"Yes, Joseph, but I don't believe there is no hope. It's just a virus, and they find cures for viruses every day."

"I wish I could be as hopeful as you. But I know my body is shutting down. But before it does, I wanted to see you, so you would understand why I left, and so I could learn how my girls are doing. I also have some things I have to give you."

"What about your friends—Donald, Melvin—"

"No one knows I'm here," he interrupted. "Nor do I want them to know."

JOSEPH

Just as Lora was about to ask more questions, Nurse Richards came in. "I'm sorry, Mr. Jones, Mrs. Jones, but it is well past visiting hours. My shift is about over, and the night nurse is not going to allow you to stay any longer."

Lora and Joseph looked at each other. "I'll be back first thing in the morning," Lora assured him as she stood up, giving him a gentle kiss. Just as she and Nurse Richards exited the room, the night nurse came in to care for Joseph.

As Lora and Nurse Richards walked to the nurses' station, Lora asked her if she knew of a nearby hotel. She said there was a facility in walking distance affiliated with the hospital that accommodates patients' families for a nominal cost. Nurse Richards called the facility, made a reservation for Lora and gave her the address. She also gave Lora a packet containing herbal tea bags. "Take this. It will help you relax and sleep. The hotel facility has a kitchen area where you can prepare it."

◆ ◆ ◆

Thanks to the herbal tea, Lora was able to fall asleep quickly. She arrived at the hospital early the next morning. Before going to Joseph's room, she went to the gift shop to get flowers. She noticed a small chess set and bought that too. She thought about calling Mama J and the girls, but decided to wait a little later, knowing that it was still early.

"Hello, I am Lora Jones, here to see my husband, Joseph Jones," Lora said to the attendant at the nurses' station.

"I'm sorry, Mrs. Jones, but visiting hours do not start until 9:00 am. If you'd like, there is a lounge and cafeteria on the first floor where you can wait until then."

Lora realized she had not eaten anything since leaving home and thought it would be good to get something to eat, even though she did not have an appetite. She found a seat by a window. While she nibbled on the bagel and sipped some orange juice, she thought about the things she and Joseph were going to discuss. She felt that it was important to know how he might have contracted the virus, but felt it was more important that they talk about their girls. She pulled out her wallet, which was loaded with pictures. She thought about the many stories that she could tell him. She thought about how proud he would be of her for buying a house. Yes! These are the things they must talk about. Positive things. She wondered what he would tell her about why he left, but she was not going to speculate. She felt that for whatever reason it was, she must be able to forgive. She looked at her watch that now read 8:30, and decided to call Mama J. She found a telephone booth in a quiet area just outside the cafeteria.

"Hello, Mama J...I'm okay, how are the girls... yes, critical, not likely...a matter of days...a flu

Joseph

virus…not now, I'll talk to them later, I need to go see him now. I'll call you this evening." Lora's better judgment was to not tell Mama J it was AIDS. She headed back up to the intensive care unit. As she arrived, she saw that Nurse Richards was now on duty.

"Hi, Lora. I'm glad you're here. Joseph is doing well this morning and he's asking for you. Did the tea help?"

"Tremendously. Thank you so much. Can I see him now?"

"Yes. Go on to his room. If you'd like, I can arrange for a wheelchair and you can take him to the top floor—the penthouse lounge with a view of the skyline. It is a very nice area."

"That sounds nice. By the way, how long has he been here?"

"He was in outpatient care for six months. He has been an intensive care patient for almost a month, which is longer than most patients. Go now—go see your husband."

As Lora entered, Joseph said, "Well good morning, my pretty lady. Come sit."

Lora placed the flowers and chess set on the nightstand. But rather than sitting on the chair, she flopped next to him on the bed and gave him a soft kiss.

"Good morning to you too, handsome."

"Me not handsome anymore," he said, amused by her trying to flatter him. "But thank you anyway," he said with a smile.

"Have you had breakfast?" she asked, observing the untouched tray of food on the cart near his bed.

"Lora, I do not mean to pain you, but I no longer eat because my body is shutting down and it can no longer sustain food. But my mind is still good. I want you to feed it by telling me about the girls and how you have been doing."

For the next hour or so, Lora told Joseph about the girls. She showed him the photos in her wallet. She told him how they spoke in unison and how they were so close, yet so different in personality and temperament. Cecilia was vivacious and talkative, and Veronica was reserved and a listener. While they often disagreed on things, they never fought and were never mean to each other. They were both accepted into the gifted program at school, but Veronica was the studious one and Cecilia the creative one. Veronica was left handed and Cecilia right handed. Cecilia liked to dress fancy, whereas Veronica liked to dress conservatively. Nonetheless, they were two peas in a pod and she did not know what they would do without each other.

Joseph looked again at their pictures and said, "Maybe we should have named them Ying and Yang." Lora burst out laughing, not only because she found it funny but because she was so glad to know that Joseph had not lost his wit and sense of humor.

While Lora did not elaborate on the house, she told Joseph that she bought a modest house in a safe neighborhood with nice neighbors, and that she was teaching the girls to play tennis.

"Is there a man in your life, Lora?" he asked in a gentle voice.

"No," she replied, saddened that he was asking this question.

"Well, I think you should—"

"Shh," she whispered, as she kissed him again softly on his parched lips.

Nurse Richards cracked the door open, peeped in and asked, "Do you want to take that ride to the penthouse lounge?"

"Joseph, it's time for you to get out of this bed," Lora commanded. "Come on in, Nurse Richards."

The nurse brought in a wheelchair and a thick robe and slippers. She and Lora dressed Joseph and helped him into the wheelchair. An orderly came and took Lora and Joseph to the penthouse lounge with views of the New York skyline. Lora brought the chess set along.

"It has been so long since I have seen the sky," Joseph said as he looked out the windows.

"And when is the last time you played a good game of chess?" Lora asked as she set up the chess game on the tray that fit to the wheelchair for patients to eat, and pulled up a nearby chair for her to sit.

Lora had never beaten Joseph in a game of chess, and even with his fragile fingers and weak condition, he was still the master as he easily took her pawns, rooks, knights. But while her queen was there for the taking, he stopped and told her he'd had enough of the game.

"Lora, it is now that I must speak to you about the unpleasant things. I beg of you to not ask me more than I am about to now tell you. Whatever questions you may have will be answered later. I have arranged for my body to be cremated, the cost of which I have already paid. I wish my ashes to be sent to you. If you consent, I would like them to be scattered over the Atlantic, where the waters will take them to my home—Jamaica. I have left an insurance policy that I took out when the girls were born. Later, I tried to get a larger policy, but it was denied because of my condition. Please use that money for whatever you need. I hope it will be enough for you to put away some for the girls' education. I intended to tell you in person why I left you and the girls. While I do not want to take a cowardly way out, I have waited too long as now I am too weak. It is too complicated to tell. However, I did write a letter about a month ago, thinking that I was going to mail it to you."

As he looked at Lora with the love he had always had for her, his eyes were filled with tears. But like most in the last stage of dying, he was not able to shed them.

"One last thing I want to say, Lora. I am confident the girls will have a good future despite not having a father. However, you, Lora, need to include a man in your life. But make sure that you truly know him before you commit yourself to him. Please, Lora."

As the tears rolled down Lora's cheeks, he took from the box of tissues a tissue and wiped her eyes. "I need some rest now, Pretty Lady. Please take me back to my room." She found a nearby attendant to assist her.

When they arrived back in the room, Lora assisted Nurse Richards in getting Joseph back into bed. She took his pulse and Lora straightened the covers on Joseph.

"I am leaving now, Joseph. But before I leave, I just want to ask you one question. Did I ever truly know you—Joseph, John, Jeremiah, Joshua, Jonah, Job, Joel, Judd Jones? Don't answer now, we will talk tomorrow. I love you," she said, giving him a gentle kiss goodnight.

As Lora exited the room, Joseph closed his eyes and whispered "I love you too."

The afternoon was still early. Instead of going back to her room at the facility, Lora hailed a cab and went to the clinic where the hospital had referred her to be tested for AIDS. She filled out some forms and then was administered the test.

She was told that the results would not be ready for two weeks. She requested that they be mailed to her if she could not pick them up. She was given several pamphlets that they advised her to read. She then took the subway to Times Square.

As she walked amongst the sardine-packed crowd, she remembered the invisibility that she felt when she first came to New York. This time she wondered about the invisibility of others, as well as herself, who might be infected with AIDS.

She half-heartedly bought some souvenirs for the girls from a street vendor. She picked up a sub sandwich and orange juice from a deli, even though she still had no appetite. The one thing that she appreciated was that the weather had been kind. She saw a peep of sunshine while looking up at the Times Square clock that now read 4:30 — a good time to call the girls. "Taxi, taxi," she called out, heading back to the facility.

Lora felt emotionally drained and confused. Thoughts tumbled through her head: "Am I happy to see Joseph, or unhappy knowing that he is dying? Should I be worried about how he got AIDS, or when he is going to die — tomorrow, next week, a miracle — he not going to die? What is he going to tell me about why he left? Or do I no longer care? After all, he did come back to me." The one thing that Lora was not confused about was that she still loved Joseph.

JOSEPH

When she arrived back at the facility, she called Mama J. They talked briefly, and then she talked to the girls. They insisted on knowing when she was coming home, reminding her that school was starting up again soon. They told her how good they were getting on the trampoline, that Danny had taught them so many card tricks, that they helped Mama J make sweet potato pie and that Ms. Lucy did their hair that morning. Thinking about the souvenirs, Lora told them she was bringing them back a present. They both shouted so loud that Lora almost dropped the phone: "A dog!?"

She took a shower and changed into her pajamas. She thought about reading the pamphlets the clinic had given her, but decided she had had enough of this matter for the day. Instead, she organized her suitcase that she so hurriedly packed. She took out the green wool turtleneck sweater that Joseph had given her one Christmas, brown tweed slacks and fresh underwear for the next day, and then packed everything else back neatly. As she was zipping up the suitcase, she saw a bulge in the side zippered pocket. She opened it and discovered a small Bible. She wondered where it came from. "Mama J, of course," she silently answered.

She lay down and opened it to Psalms and read the scriptures. *A father to the fatherless, a defender of widows, is God in his holy dwelling. God sets the lonely in families...* She fell asleep with the small Bible in her hands, forgetting to eat the sub sandwich.

At 9:55 that night, she was awakened by the ringing telephone. She answered. It was Nurse Richards.

"I'm coming now," Lora replied as she put on her coat over her pajamas."

Joseph had died at 9:45 pm.

Her legs, which felt like cement when she first arrived at the hospital, now felt like mush as she walked down the long corridor to the intensive care unit nurses' station.

"I am Mrs. Lora Jones, here to see my husband, patient Joseph J. Jones," she said for the last time.

That night before leaving the hospital, Nurse Richards gave her a large envelope that Joseph had left in his nightstand for her. Lora asked Nurse Richards why Joseph died so quickly after having the stamina to get into the wheelchair, go to the penthouse lounge, play chess and have a long conversation with her?

Nurse Richards answer was not from a medical perspective. Rather it was her personal opinion from her 20 years of experience as a nurse. "Perhaps because, like they say, *a lightbulb is it's brightest before it burns out.* And perhaps he had done the one thing he was staying alive to do—to see and talk with you one more time. There was a peacefulness about him when he died."

❖ ❖ ❖

JOSEPH

When Lora returned to the facility, she changed from her pajamas to the clothes she had laid out in anticipation of seeing Joseph the next day, and packed up to leave. She paid the attendant the remainder of the bill, who called a taxi to take her to Penn Station. She then asked the attendant if she could borrow the phone.

"Mama J, Joseph passed. I am taking the midnight train home to Georgia. I should be there tomorrow evening, around 7."

Lora asked a porter if she could sit where she would have no one seated next to her. She wanted solitude. The porter gladly obliged. As the train blew its whistle, pulled out of the station and accelerated its speed once it hit open terrain, she sat back and opened the envelope, which had a mailing label on it with her name and address. She then wondered how he knew her address, and the hospital had her telephone number, since she had moved. Probably because she was listed, she thought. But it didn't matter; there were too many other questions that she had not asked and that he had not answered—especially why he had left her.

In the large envelope were three smaller ones, and on one of them was written in his handwriting, *Open Me Last*. She opened the first blank envelope and it was an insurance policy for $100,000 payable to her as beneficiary. She opened the second blank envelope. It had Polaroid shots from the surprise birthday party she had thrown him and a picture of him and her with the girls when they were first born. Also, there in a folded handkerchief, was his wedding ring that she had engraved with all of his initials—nine Js. She then opened the *Open Me Last* envelope.

> *My Dearest Lora,*
>
> *As you read this letter, I want you to know that I did love you, and still do as I write this now. As a matter of fact, I think I love you more now than when I married you, however strange this may sound as you read what I am about to reveal.*
>
> *I am gay, Lora, always have been. While I was attracted to men at an early age, I never acted on these urges. In my mind and heart, it was sinful, and taboo in the Jamaican culture. Instead, I became very promiscuous with women, trying to show the world and myself that I was indeed a man. But shortly before I met you, I gave in to my hidden desire and had my first experience with a man. I could not deny the pleasure that I felt, which was greater than I had ever experienced with a woman. However, I felt dirty, cheap, sinful. I tried to convince myself that if only I met the right woman, this curse in my body would go away. Then I met you. In my heart, you fulfilled me more than anyone I had ever met. You fulfilled my body desires as well, but I still had that yearning and lust for a man.*

Joseph

When the girls were born, I felt even more shame and guilt. My friends would say things, like "you the man, got dem soldiers to make twins." One day, as I was coming home from work, I was approached by a man who asked me for a date. I was so attracted to him, and my lust for him was almost overpowering, but I declined. This was the day that I decided I would rather leave you than cheat on you, especially in this sinful way. The next day, I went and sold my watch and the gold chain necklace my mother had given to me, and I bought a one-way ticket to a town in Italy that accepted gays. Then, when I found out I had AIDS, I came back to New York for treatment, and was hoping to see you before I died, to make this confession.

I hope someday you will forgive me, as I cannot forgive myself—for deceiving you, for not taking care of our girls.

While God may not forgive me, I hope he will answer my one prayer, and that is that you and the girls will always have angels by your sides, to protect you as long as you live.

Goodbye, my Pretty Lady,

Love, Joseph

Now Lora knew the answer to the question that she had asked herself for nearly five years—why he left. She also knew the answer to the question she last asked Joseph before he died: "Did I ever truly know you?"

Medical experts say that when the body receives pain that is too traumatic for the nerves, the body goes into shock whereby one feels no pain, no sensation. And so it was with Lora. But it was not physical, but her emotions. All she felt was emptiness.

CHAPTER VI

The Wait

"Your Mommy will be home soon, but she is very tired, so I want you to let her get some rest," Mama J told the girls. She knew that Lora would be in a somber state when she returned home. But it was to no avail, as the girls ran out screaming with delight as soon as they saw their mother climb out of the cab. Their screaming alerted the rest of the neighbors that Lora was home. Edna and Big Lucy went to their front door and waved to Lora. Danny watched her from his bedroom window and was glad to see her. But like Mama J, everyone's discretion said not to bombard her with greetings or questions. Mama J walked over and gave Lora the house keys, and told her that she prepared dinner and had left it in Lora's kitchen, for her to get some rest—it was almost 7 pm—and that they could talk tomorrow.

Lora was relieved. Although happy to be home and to see Mama J, she did not want to engage in conversation at that time, and she knew the girls would want her undivided attention. They did indeed as they asked for the first time in a long while, "Mommy can we sleep with you tonight?"

As the girls nestled on each side of her that night, she wondered about the day when she would have to tell them the truth about their father. She also wondered about what she would tell the ladies—surely not the truth.

The following morning, Lora called Mama J and asked if they could talk that afternoon, that she would make some tea, and that she was inviting Edna and Big Lucy as well. Edna said that Danny could keep the girls occupied while they talked. Lora said she thought that would be a good idea. It was too cold that day for the trampoline, so Danny challenged the girls to a game of checkers at his house, while the ladies talked in the quiet of Lora's living room.

"He died as a result of a flu virus," she told them. Lora decided not to reveal that Joseph had died from AIDS, and that she might be infected. She also did not reveal to them Joseph's secret of being gay. One mistruth led to another.

"He left me for another woman, and they moved to Europe. He realized he had made a mistake, but felt that I would not forgive him. But when he found out he was dying, he called me because he wanted to tell me the truth and to ask for my forgiveness." Lora felt worse and worse as she lied to the ladies. But what else could she do? She had to tell them something, she rationalized. She knew the ladies were just waiting to express their loathing for what Joseph had done to her, and that they were probably thinking he deserved to die. Maybe not Mama J, but she probably didn't feel much sympathy for him either.

In an attempt to subdue their animosity, she showed them the pictures that Joseph had left her. "He also still had his wedding ring, something most men get rid if they no longer care." This still did not seem to evoke any sympathy from the ladies.

"He expressed that he had prayed for God's forgiveness, but he felt he did not deserve it for the wrong he had done. He prayed to God that me and the girls would be protected by angels." This seemed to appease Mama J.

Then Lora told them about the $100,000 insurance policy. "He said he that he tried to get a higher policy but was declined because of his health condition." This seemed to impress all the ladies.

Mama J sensed Lora's uneasiness, attributing it to the long journey and all the turmoil she went through. So she took the initiative of ending the conversation and suggested to the ladies that they all leave now so Lora could get some rest.

As they left, Lora thanked the ladies for looking after the girls and all that they had done for her. She felt relieved but still guilty for having to lie to the ladies—her friends, people who trusted her.

◆ ◆ ◆

The holidays were over and the neighborhoods were busy with the tedious task of taking down Christmas lights. The yellow school buses were back on the road, and highways were filled with people going back to work. On the road, too, was a new driver—Danny, who just got his license. The Saturday before school had started again, Walter drove up in a new silver gray Fleetwood Cadillac. Danny and Edna came out to meet him.

"Well, we finally have our dream car, Walter," Edna said with pride. "Ain't got that mahogany door, but I'm not complaining," she said gleefully.

Walter turned to Danny. "Here you go, son, the keys to the old car, as I promised you," Walter said. "Take care of it, and it will take care of you. That means checking the fluids regularly, especially the oil, and make sure you rotate the tires every six months, and always make sure your brakes are working properly. I already put you on the insurance policy. Like I told you, just one ticket—I mean just one—and I'm taking back the keys."

"Thanks, Dad, I really appreciate this. And tomorrow I am going to wash and wax it," Danny said as he was also calculating how much a new paint job would cost.

"Get in, baby, let's take a ride," Walter said as Edna flopped into the front seat passenger side, almost forgetting that she had left oxtails cooking on the stove. "Danny, turn off the stove."

That Friday, Lora cashed her paycheck. After getting home, she went to Mama J's to pay her back the money that made it possible for her to go New York—which was nearly Lora's full week's salary. She also made sure to let Mama J know that she would pay for the collect calls as soon as Mama J got the bill.

Then Lora asked, "Mama J, what do you think about me getting the girls a dog?"

"Well, having a dog is like having a child. You got to feed it, get it shots, keep it clean and give it a lot of lovin' if you really care about it."

"How come no one else in the neighborhood has a dog?" Lori asked.

"Edna and Walter never had one, don't know why. Maybe because Edna wants everything so neat and clean. Mr. Felix ain't had no dog, probably because he's just too mean. Big Lucy and Milky had a German Shepard name Bruno, but he got hit by a car. I had three dogs when my children were growing up. Snow White was the mama. She had a litter. I kept a boy and a girl, Silver and Pepper. Snow White died when she was 16; buried her in the backyard at the old house. Anyone who says dogs don't mourn is badly mistakin' 'cause Silver and Pepper stayed there by her grave every day for nearly a month. Silver died from dog diabetes, the vet said. Pepper died about six months later. I think it was from a broken heart, missin' Silver. Losin' them was too painful. That's why I didn't get another. But I do think that everyone should have a dog in their lifetime. They show you—what's that word?" Mama J paused and then answered her own question, "Yeah, unconditional love."

"Mama J, when I was leaving for New York and asked you who would be looking after the girls, you said you—their godmother. Did you mean that? I mean about being their godmother?"

"Well, given my age, I would not be the best one to be their godmother, but until you find someone more suitable, I would like to be."

"I would like you to be. As their godmother, I need to talk to you about some things. So if you don't mind, can we talk after church on Sunday?"

"That's a good time for me, a very appropriate time, Lora," Mama J said as she thought maybe it would also be a good time to approach Lora about the girls attending church with her.

"I better get back. I told the girls I would only be gone a minute." As Lora was about to enter her house, she noticed a package about the size of a shoe box next to the door. It was from the cemetery—Joseph's ashes. While the box was carefully wrapped and shrink wrapped, she was irritated that something so important was not sent special delivery. She put the box in the china cabinet drawer where she had earlier put Joseph's wedding ring and the letter he had written to her.

On Saturday evening, Lora went over the information she received from various banks and investment firms that she had contacted, and made a list of things she wanted to talk with Mama J about on Sunday.

That Sunday morning, the girls woke Lora, gleefully saying, "Mommy, Mommy, wake up, it's snowing!" While the dusting of snow was too light for them to make a snowman, the girls and Lora got dressed in their winter wear and went outside to play in the soft accumulation of snowflakes.

During breakfast, Lora asked the girls about getting a pet, and they adamantly said they wanted a dog.

"Well, what about a cat? How about a hamster, or maybe a fish?"

"Nah, a dog."

"If you had a dog what would you want, a boy or girl, and why?"

"A girl, we can paint her toenails, and make pretty hats for her," answered Cecelia.

"A boy, because we don't have any boys in our family," countered Veronica.

"And what would you name her or him, and why?"

"Happy," said Cecelia, "because we would be so happy, and she would be so happy."

"No, Lucky", said Veronica, "because he is going to bring us lots of luck. He can dig in the yard and find gold."

"Which name do you like best, Mommy? Happy or Lucky?"

"I like both. What about the name Happy Go Lucky?"

"Mommy, Mommy, that's a great name! Yay! So that means we get a dog?"

"No, I just asked you if you wanted one. How about a play dog, the kind you can wind up to walk and bark?"

"Ahh, that's not fair, Mommy."

"Enough talk about dogs, clear this table, and I want you to get in your room and clean it up, it's a mess. And Ms. Lucy is expecting you to come over this afternoon and help her pack some things to take to the homeless shelter."

"Mommy, I saw a commercial the other day that showed a lot of dogs that are homeless," said Veronica.

While the girls were at Big Lucy's helping pack items for the homeless, Lora and Mama J talked in the privacy of Lora's dining room.

"Mama J, the reason I don't use this as a china cabinet is, well for one, because I don't have any china, and two, and more importantly, I keep in it things that are very important to me. This key locks all the doors and drawers. I keep it way on top of the cabinet so that no one can find it, and so that I don't misplace it," Lora said, as she stood on top of a footstool to get the key.

"In this drawer are Joseph's wedding ring and ashes. Someday I want to have the ashes scattered over the Atlantic Ocean as he requested. In this drawer are photos of me and my adoptive parents, and photos of me, Joseph and the girls when we were a family. I don't frame them and put them on display because they bring back too many bitter memories. And in this drawer are important papers: the bill of sale for the house, my and the girls' birth certificates and the insurance policy that Joseph left." Lora took out the insurance policy.

"With the $100,000, I am going to open for each of the girls an education fund of $40,000 each. By the time they are 18, they will have yielded $10,000 in interest, so that means they will both have $50,000 each for their college education. I'm putting $15,000 into a savings account for any medical emergencies. This will leave $5,000 to finish repairs and things I need for the house. I'm also looking into taking out a life insurance policy in case something happens to me." Seeing that Mama J was getting confused with all the figures and terminology, Lora noted that everything would be put in writing.

"Cecilia and Veronica have no relatives, being that I was adopted, and Joseph was an only child, raised by his mother who is no longer alive. That means if I die, they most likely would become wards of the state. So, if anything were to happen to me, I want to ask you, as their godmother, would take care of them, or find them a good home?"

Lora was now talking Mama J's language, as Mama J recalled how she was so worried while raising her kids as a single parent, and what would happen to them if she died.

"Lora, thank you for trustin' me with this information, and 'specially the care of the girls. I know nothing is going to happen to you, but if it does, rest assured, I will carry out your wishes. But there is something I must ask you. If something happens to you, can I please take the girls to church? And I was even thinking, maybe once in a while, they can start going to church with me now."

"Mama J, if something happens to me, and you're raising them, I would expect and want them to go to church with you. And yes, if you want them to go to church with you on Sundays, that's fine, too. The only thing I request is that you never teach them that other religions are wrong. I want them to judge people by their acts, not by their religion."

The conversation ended as Cecilia and Veronica came bursting through the door, bragging about how well they helped Ms. Lucy and Mr. Milky pack the boxes for the homeless shelter.

"Mama J, your hat is so pretty," Veronica said as she felt the flower and satin bow.

"It's my church hat," replied Mama J.

"Can we go to church with you someday?" Veronica softly asked.

Lora and Mama J looked at one another with the same thought: "Isn't this a coincidence."

"Yes you can," Mama J said as she gave Veronica a big hug.

The Wait

As Lora left the next day for work, she gave Walter a thumbs up as he was getting into his new Cadillac. While she drove she made mental notes of what she had to do that week—call the insurance company, a lawyer, the investment firms and banks. She'd have to do it on her lunch hour, she thought. She'd use the telephone booth just outside the café. But the mental note that was foremost in her mind was to check the mailbox for the AIDS test results. It had been over two weeks.

When she arrived home that day with the girls and opened the mailbox, there was the envelope, marked *Confidential, for Addressee Only*. She instructed the girls to go to their room and start their homework, not to disturb her as she had something very important to do. Lora went to the confines of her bedroom, shut the door, sat on the bed. "Mama J, you tell me to put my faith in Jesus, and to pray. I'm doing that right now," she said silently as she opened the envelope. The test results indicated that she was negative. Tears of relief filled her eyes. "Thank you Dear Jesus. Thank Dear God."

The next day, Lora left work early and went to the ASPCA, and brought home Happy Go Lucky.

CHAPTER VII

New Relationships

Of all the dogs in the shelter that Lora could have chosen, Happy Go Lucky got her attention. He was about three months old and in a cage with five other puppies. They were of the same litter. A mixed breed—a little bit of cocker spaniel, golden retriever and yorkie. When Lora looked in their cage, the other puppies jumped up and barked at her, while Happy Go Lucky just sat there and looked at her. When she left their cage to look at other dogs, the five puppies stopped barking and paid no further attention to her. But Happy Go Lucky stood up then, went to the front of the cage and did not take his eyes off of Lora as she circled the room looking at the other dogs. She looked back at Happy Go Lucky's cage and he was still standing and looking at her. He gave her a soft yelp. Lora asked the attendant, "Why does he yelp rather than bark?" The attendant explained that when a dog yelps, it usually is a sign of pain, or that it needs help. "I'll take him," she told the attendant.

While the girls had the pleasure of his company and playing with Happy Go Lucky, they also had the responsibility of taking care of him: feeding, bathing, walking and training him not to relieve himself in the house. "Why can't we just put diapers on him?" Cecilia said, as she was cleaning up the puddle he made in the living room. Lora was glad that she had hardwood floors in the living room because that is where most of his accidents happened. Had it been carpet, it would have been so much harder to clean—not to mention the lingering smell.

Because there were no leash laws, and they lived in a cu-de-sac with no traffic, Happy Go Lucky would often run free in the neighborhood when the girls played outside. The neighbors befriended him by giving him doggie treats as he frequently sniffed the tree trunks and bushes in everyone's yard, marking his territory by lifting his hind leg and relieving himself. Lora and the girls made sure to scoop up his poop, but sometimes he would do it where it was camouflaged in the dirt and grass in all the yards. The neighbors didn't mind. They thought it made good fertilizer, just as long as they did not step on it.

Cecilia and Veronica asked Danny if he could teach Happy Go Lucky tricks like he had taught them card tricks. Danny went to the library and got a book on how to do this and became a hero in the girls' eyes by teaching Happy Go Lucky to sit, kneel, roll over, jump. But the trick they liked best was when Danny would say "Give me your paw," Happy Go Lucky would extend it for Danny to shake.

The girls asked Lora if they could make a doggie door in her mahogany door for him to go in and out. Lora looked at them as if they were crazy. She didn't think they were too crazy though when she saw the scratches on the inside of the door that Happy Go Lucky made one day when the girls were late in taking him out. Lora called a handyman the next day who installed a doggie door leading out to the carport.

◆ ◆ ◆

Happy Go Lucky would not be the only new relationship in Lora's life. It was in early February that Lora met Frank.

It was time for Lora's half-hour lunch break when she headed to her usual place—a café two doors away—and ordered her usual sub and a glass of orange juice. As she ate her lunch, reading an article about new techniques in horticulture, she was interrupted.

"Hello, may I join you?" the stranger asked.

Lora looked around and saw that the café was crowded, and she should not monopolize a whole table that was designed for two, so she did not object. "Okay," she answered nonchalantly, and continued reading her article as if he were not there.

"I see that you work at the nursery a couple of doors down," he said observing the company t-shirt she was wearing. "I'm Frank Parker, one of your customers. My firm does a lot of business with your company," he said while sipping his coffee.

This did get Lora's attention, as the name Parker rang a bell—a big bell if it was Parker Real Estate Development—one of the nursery's major customers. He handed Lora one of his business cards.

"Yes, I am familiar with your company. My name is Lora Jones. Nice to meet you."

"What is your association with the nursery, may I ask?'

"Horticulturalist—cultivating and making sure the plants are healthy."

"Well, you must be doing an excellent job, because all the plants we buy from your nursery are far superior to plants from anywhere else."

"Why, thank you. That is quite a compliment." Lora glanced at her watch and saw that it was time she got back to work. "I have to go now, but it was a pleasure meeting you."

"You as well, *Miss*—or is it *Missus*?" he asked as he looked at her hand for a wedding ring, thinking he cannot be sure—that perhaps she is not wearing a wedding band because of the nature of her work.

Lora usually answered this question with *Missus*, perhaps out of habit or knowingly because she did not want the attention of someone. But this time she answered *Miss*—Miss Lora Jones.

For the next several weeks, at least three times a week, Frank Parker would make it a point to go to the café in the hope of meeting Lora there, and most of the time she was there. During their meetings, they talked about plants, landscaping and the weather. Frank had a way of making the most mundane topics seem interesting. But tidbits of personal information started to be shared as the meetings became regular.

Lora shared that she was widowed and the mother of two girls, that she had been living in Augusta for about five years, that she purchased a home about a year ago, that she had a dog. When she told him the name, he thought it amusing and asked how it got that name. She told him the story, and he found that even more amusing.

He shared with her that he was single, no kids. He attributed that to being too busy building his company, but he was only 36, and felt he had plenty of time for that in the future. His company and home was in Atlanta, but he also owned an apartment in Augusta because of the frequent trips he had to make there for business purposes.

A week went by during which Frank did not show up at the café. As she was leaving work that Friday, however, the receptionist told Lora that she'd received a package that was delivered by courier. She went to her car and opened it. It was a box of Godiva chocolates, packaged with a note.

> *Dear Lora, I truly missed your sweet smile and conversation this past week. I would like to take you to dinner at a restaurant in Augusta this Saturday around 8:00 pm. Please call me if you will do me the honor. Frank.*

Enclosed with the note was his business card and on the back were his home and beeper numbers.

After she got home from work and the girls were settled, she thought about the invitation and decided to accept, but wondered who would watch the girls? First to come to mind was Mama J, but she felt that would be too late on any given night for her to stay up. So she went over to ask Edna, who usually stayed up late.

"Of course I will. It's about time you went out on a date. As a matter of fact, why don't you let the girls spend the night? The girls will probably be asleep before you get home, and you won't have to wake them up. What time is he picking you up?"

"I think it's best that I meet him, rather than him coming here. Reservation is for 8, so I'll need to leave here at 7:30-ish."

Edna was somewhat disappointed that Lora's date was not picking her up, because she wanted to meet the man. Nonetheless, she thought it was wise on Lora's part to meet him at the restaurant rather than him coming to Lora's house since she, Edna assumed, had only recently met him.

That Saturday, after the tennis lesson with the girls, Lora told them they would be having a sleep over at Ms. Edna's house. They thought that would be exciting, and asked if Happy Go Lucky could come too? She called Edna, who said that was fine. After dinner, she told the girls to take a bath, put on their PJs and to get a book and game that they wanted to take to the sleep over.

Lora then went to her room to get dressed. She decided to wear a knee length, simple black dress that she had not worn since her separation from Joseph. She accessorized it with a pair of cubic zirconia stud earrings, a small silver brooch and black patent leather three-inch heels. At 7:30 she headed to Edna's with the girls, in their PJs, and Happy Go Lucky wagging his tail.

Edna told her she looked lovely, that the girls would be just fine, to have a good time, to drive safely and to call her if anything went wrong. Danny came into the living room as they were talking. He was taken back by how stunning Lora looked. He had never seen her dressed up or in heels. He hid his admiration while he picked up and petted Happy Go Lucky, and asked the girls what games they wanted to play that evening.

Lora arrived at the restaurant about 10 minutes late because she couldn't find a parking spot. She did not know that there was valet service. Frank sat in the lobby waiting for her. He dismissed her apology for being late with a soft kiss on her cheek, as the maître d' escorted them to their table.

While Lora had been to some swanky restaurants, it was usually as hired help to set up floral displays. As she looked at Frank, she thought how he fit so well in the posh environment—suave and sophisticated, dressed like he just came out of *Gentleman's Quarterly* magazine.

Frank asked her what her wine preference was. She told him that she had none because she did not drink, but not to let that stop him. He declined as well, and told the sommelier, "Thank you, but no thank you." He was somewhat disappointed that Lora did not drink because he wanted her in a relaxed state of mind.

As they ate their lavish meal, the conversation was more romantic than the conversations they had during Lora's lunch break at the café. He complimented Lora on how lovely she looked, and told her the things that attracted him to her—her graceful manner, her quiet yet confident demeanor, her skill as a horticulturist. He talked about his travels to Europe, Rio de Janeiro and the Caribbean—places that he hoped to take someone special someday. Lora knew he was trying to woo her and perhaps laying it on thick, but she didn't mind a bit. He then asked what impressed her about a man? Her answer was someone who could make her laugh. He anticipated this. It was the answer that he got from most of the women he dated, and he had come up with a response that women found amusing, as did Lora. He pulled from his Armani sports jacket a small paperback book entitled *1000 Best Jokes* and read Lora some jokes. Lora did not need any wine that evening. Frank's attention to her was intoxicating enough.

◆ ◆ ◆

Seeing that the girls were getting sleepy, Danny opened the living room convertible sofa and made it up with Edna's spare linen. After they were tucked in, he read them a story from one of the books they brought over. Before he was halfway finished, they were sound asleep, as was Happy Go Lucky at the foot of the sofa bed. He went into the family room where Edna and Walter were watching a movie, told them that the girls were asleep and he was headed up to his room.

He wondered about how well he had done on his pre-collegiate exams, he thought about what color he was going to paint his car and he thought about how beautiful Lora looked that evening.

His thoughts would not let him sleep, so he got up, put on some sneakers, got his tennis racket and the tube of tennis balls he had bought and went out to the back of his house. When Danny was four, Walter converted the yard into an area where he and Danny could play basketball. It included a six-foot-wide, eight-foot-tall wooden fence. Danny played tennis with the fence until he heard the sound of the motor as Lora pulled into her driveway. It was almost mid-night. He was glad she had made it home safely.

◆ ◆ ◆

Frank's business in Augusta became less demanding while his business in Atlanta required more of his attention. Therefore, his and Lora's afternoon visits at the café pretty much ceased. So Frank asked Lora if they could see each other on the weekends. The evenings were problematic for Lora because she did not want to impose on Edna to watch the girls every weekend, and Mama J and Big Lucy retired early. Frank suggested hiring a babysitter, and that he would pay the cost, but Lora was not agreeable to the girls staying with strangers. Frank was becoming a little annoyed, and thought perhaps Lora was not that interested in seeing him. Also, Lora had never invited him to her house. So, he confronted her with his concerns, and in doing so told her that he was serious about their relationship. He wrote this to her in a letter, and had it hand couriered to the nursery with a box of Godiva chocolates that Friday.

> *Lora, I find you fascinating and want to spend much more time with you. I understand and respect your obligations and responsibilities as a*

mother. But, if we are to cultivate our relationship, I need you to find a way and time to be with me. Please let me know your thoughts. Affectionately yours, Frank.

Lora called him that evening, and invited him over to her house on that Sunday for an early dinner.

The ladies were buzzing about Lora's new dating life, so that Saturday, after the men had cut the yards, and Lora and the girls returned from playing tennis, they called her over to Mama J's house, and point-blank asked her about her new relationship — who, when, how they met?

Lora gave them enough details to satisfy their curiosity, and told them she thought she might want to cultivate the relationship.

"Well, when can we meet this young man?"

"He is coming over tomorrow evening," she replied. "But I don't think it will be a good time for you to meet him. I think it would look childish if I introduce you all to him the first time he comes over. And I think it will seem like I'm too anxious — plus I don't want him to think that he is so important that I have to introduce him to my neighbors so soon." After pondering a bit, the ladies concurred that Lora was absolutely right.

While the girls were at church with Mama J, Lora cooked a pot roast with roasted potatoes and fixed a Caesar salad. For dessert, she made a peach cobbler. She set the table for four with a white linen table cloth and matching napkins. She had bought a set of dinnerware that looked as nice as real china, and glasses that simulated crystal. The utensils were not as impressive, but would have to do. She made a small round centerpiece with cut flowers and ferns. She thought to put some candles on the table but changed her mind. This was not intended to be a romantic dinner. It was for him to meet the girls, and to see where and how she lived. It was to cultivate their relationship, not consummate it.

Frank arrived promptly at 5 o'clock. While he was dressed casually in khaki pants, and a dark brown V-neck cashmere sweater, he still looked "GQ." He brought three red roses and carried a small gift bag. Lora introduced him to the girls and he handed both a rose, as he told them it was a pleasure to meet them. The largest rose he handed to Lora. Then he opened the small gift bag which had a small, pre-cooked filet mignon and said, "This is for Happy Go Lucky," who, hearing his name, came running out from the girls' room.

While the food turned out as well as could be expected, the conversation at the dinner table was a bit awkward. Frank tried to engage the girls in conversation, but they seemed disinterested. He tried to tell them a joke, but it went as flat and dry as an overcooked pancake. Lora found the uneasiness of the usually suave, composed, charming Frank humorous, and attributed it to him not having children or being around children. The girls ate their food quickly, and after their last bite of the peach cobbler, looked at their mother with a desperation that said *please can we go now*. Lora dismissed them from the table, telling them to make sure they washed their hands. Not forgetting their manners, but forgetting his name, they said, "Nice meeting you," and hurried to wash their hands and went to their room to play.

Lora and Frank spent the rest of their visit talking about cultivating their relationship. Lora said that Sundays would be a good day for them to see each other at her house. That once a month, on the weekends, her neighbor could watch the girls and they could go out. Frank asked if, when their relationship became intimate, would she be sleeping overnight with him? Lora replied that if—with the emphasis on *if*—they became intimate, that he could not spend the night at her place because of her children, but she might—with the emphasis on *might*—consider spending the night occasionally—with the emphasis on *occasionally*—at his place.

They both looked intensively at each other as they felt the physical urge to be with one another until Happy Go Lucky gave out a yelp saying he needed to relieve himself, and Lora realized it was the girls' bedtime.

As Frank headed out to his BMW, he felt the hardness of his manhood and said to himself, "Got to have that woman. Too bad she has those kids."

CHAPTER VIII

Belonging

FRANK PARKER WAS A PRODUCT OF GRANDPARents who, in the 1920s, moved from Atlanta to Chicago and passed for white, as did their children. Their children, including Frank's father, went on to marry white spouses, and their black genes became masked. However, when Frank was born, those recessive genes came out. While his skin coloring was fair, he had prominent black features—a wide nose, full lips and course hair. He was his parents' first child, and they made sure he would be their last.

While his parents weren't unkind to him, they pretty much put him in parentheses—never taking him anywhere and confining him to his bedroom when company came over. As soon as Frank graduated from high school, they shipped him off to college and told him that they would continue to support him until he graduated, but that he was now on his own—a kind way to say he need not come back home. Frank held no animosity toward them either. Rather, he put them in parentheses as well, and rarely called or visited them, knowing that this was their wish.

He liked being bi-racial — the best of both worlds, he thought. He liked his strong, manly features that he felt made him look attractive to women, and his light skin opened doors for him, especially when he processed his hair. Perhaps because of his upbringing, Frank became a loner and emotionally detached to people. But he did like the attention of others — those who admired and respected him, people who wanted to befriend him, get close to him — but only those that he could control and keep at a distance.

While he was the owner of a successful commercial property development and management company, he did not start or build it. Rather, he acquired it by marrying a woman who had inherited it herself. She was killed in a car accident six years after they were married. Frank became the sole owner. He did not want the responsibility of running the company on a day-to-day basis, so he hired highly skilled staff to manage operations, and he paid them well. However, he made sure to dress and act the executive role, making frequent visits to the operating site in Atlanta. He was adamant about reviewing contracts and approving every penny that was received and spent.

Frank did not marry his wife for her money, but it wasn't out of love either. Rather it was because it was a comfortable relationship. She was attentive to his needs and never made any demands. The money, however, did become a major factor in keeping the marriage together. After a couple years his interest in her waned, as did his physical attraction to her now plumped up body. While they were married, his wife badly wanted a child but fertility tests showed that he was sterile. She wanted to adopt, but he did not. Being sterile was of no consequence to him because he never wanted children anyway; so adoption was certainly out of the question.

Getting women was no problem for Frank. Although he was not a head-turner, he was pleasant to look at, very neat in his appearance and he exuded confidence. He gained the affection of women by the way he talked to and treated them. He listened rather than talked, observed rather than inquired. His money was a factor as well. He knew that from the way he dressed—Rolex watch, designer clothes and expensive car—he would be a magnet to gold diggers. But he had a strategy for them. He would wine and dine them, get them to be intimate and then when they would hit him up for money, jewelry or anything expensive, he would drop them like a hot potato.

However, many women that he had met were not gold diggers and wanted a sincere relationship. But they were more problematic than the gold diggers—they wanted marriage and children. Frank wanted neither. He would cater to their needs by engaging in activities that they liked, such as meeting their friends and family, going to church with them even though he was an agnostic and pretending to like their children. While Frank never led these women on, never promised them a future, he would listen to them prattle about their rose garden. He never told them that he loved them. Rather, he said that he cared—which many took as his way of expressing his love. When the relationship got too demanding, he would drop them as he did the gold diggers—like a hot potato.

Usually his relationships lasted three to four months at the most. Now though it had been close to four months since he met Lora at the café and he had not dated or talked to any other women since then. Thus far, Lora had given no indication of being a gold digger or a clinging vine. But she also was not giving him the attention that he needed—which was not only physical, but emotional as well.

◆ ◆ ◆

Mother's Day was just around the corner. Cecilia and Veronica approached Lora about an idea that they wanted to do for that day.

"Mommy, on Mother's Day we want to have a party for you and all the mothers in the neighborhood," Veronica explained.

"And me, Veronica and Mama J's grandchildren are going to do the cooking and make cards and presents, and decorate," Cecilia chimed in.

"Now the men can help too. They can go to the store and pick up everything we need. I am making a shopping list," Veronica said while holding a paper on which she had already jotted a few items—balloons, paper hats, a pony.

"And Danny can help us make barbecue chicken, ribs and hotdogs like he did last summer for Mr. Walter's birthday."

"Well, where are you going to get the money to do all this?" asked Lora who was amused yet impressed and interested.

"Selling lemonade. Our friend Patricia does it all the time at her house and one time she made $20!" Cecilia said confidently.

"Well, this is a big project and a lot to think about. So give Mommy a couple of days to think about it. Okay? Now you need to get ready for bed, and I need to go walk Happy Go Lucky."

As Lora walked the dog, she thought how nice and clever the girls' idea was, but how costly it was going to be. "Going to have do more than sell lemonade," she said to Happy Go Lucky, who gave out a yelp as if he understood.

That Friday evening, Lora talked with Mama J, Edna and Big Lucy about the idea. They all thought it was sweet, but hilarious knowing that it would be them that would end up doing the work.

"Dang," Big Lucy, exclaimed, "Let's do it. I'll be fun. I ain't no mother, but I sho feel like one since the girls moved here. Now we know those girls ain't gonna make no money selling lemonade. So why don't we get the men to fork up the money?"

"Good idea, Lucy. 'Stead of buying me flowers and that chocolate that he ends up eating, I'll tell Walter to put that money toward our party," Edna said. "And Danny always asking me what I want for Mothers' Day. Now he'll know just what I want."

"My grands are going to have so much fun doing this—for me and their mamas. A block party for all us mamas. Who would have thought about that, mmm, mm, mm," Mama J said in admiration of the girls.

Lora was happy that the ladies liked the idea. "Okay, I am going to make a list of all the things that need to be done. While we are going to end up doing most of the work, I want the kids to feel like they are in charge, since it is their party for us," Lora advised.

"I'll talk with my daughters and their husbands, who are coming over tomorrow. Lora, you can get the girls and my grands together to talk about what they want to do and supervise that end," Mama J said. She did not have the patience for this task. She could only take so much of kids loud talking and running around, as kids do. Mama J loved her grandchildren, but she was so glad when they would go back home so she could get some peace and quiet.

"I can borrow some folding tables and chairs from the homeless center. We can set them up in the middle of the cul-de-sac," Big Lucy said with excitement.

"I'll pick up plastic tablecloths for the tables, stuff we need to eat with, and take the girls to Kmart and pick up decorations," Lora said, as she heard the girls calling "Mommy, when are you coming home?" and realizing she had been gone for almost an hour and had not prepared dinner.

All the ladies had gotten so wrapped up in the conversation that they did not realize how late it was. So, Edna and Big Lucy also parted to go home and prepare dinner. Mama J went outside to check her garden to make sure there was enough collard greens for cooking.

◆ ◆ ◆

Lora thought the party would be a good time during which Frank to meet her neighbors, now that she was seeing him on a regular basis. The arrangement that they made to meet on Sundays was working very well. Even though their time was limited, it was quality time during which they had one another's undivided attention. Frank would arrive shortly after the girls left for church with Mama J. Frank, who usually was the listener, was the talker as Lora listened to him attentively about whatever was on his mind. She was impressed with his complex thinking and extensive vocabulary. Often times, when she was trying to express something but could not find the words, he would provide the exact word she wanted to say. She was surprised that he knew so much about history and current events. Most of the books that she had in her small bookshelf library he seemed to have read. When she pondered the solution to a problem, he came up with several solutions. She was impressed by his investigative eye and ability to discern situations.

What Lora did not find pleasing about Frank was his lack of compassion and concern when she expressed her empathy and sympathy for the unfortunate. He took a Darwinian, philosophical view "survival of the fittest." While this did bother her about him, she did not look at it as a flaw in his character, rather as a difference in their emotional and intellectual makeup—that she was idealistic and he was pragmatic.

Things that made Frank feel comfortable with Lora were that she never talked about marriage, religion, her finances or even very much about the girls or her aspirations for the future. Yet she was interesting because she had an inquisitive mind, one that he hoped to mold to his way of thought, to make her compatible.

But some of those things that made Frank feel comfortable with Lora also made him feel uncomfortable. He wanted to know more about her; he wanted her to be more emotionally dependent on him; he wanted her to be more submissive. He wanted her to want him more. What he wanted from her was far more than physical.

◆ ◆ ◆

It was Saturday, the day before the Mothers' Day block party, and everyone was excited and in full motion. At the crack of dawn, Walter and Danny took the long shopping list and went to buy the food, beverages and charcoal for the grills, and got back home by 9 to cut the grass. Mama J and Edna started cooking the things that could be prepared ahead of time. Mama J got out the pots, pans, trays, bowls and utensils needed for cooking and serving and started a big pot of collard greens and ham hocks. Edna started preparing the red beans and rice, potato salad and seasoned the ribs and chicken to marinate for barbecuing the next day. Big Lucy and Milky picked up the tables and chairs from the homeless shelter. Milky also borrowed a sound system with speakers to play music, and Big Lucy picked out some music—Motown hits—that both the adults and kids would enjoy.

Earlier that week, Lora took the girls to Kmart to shop for decorations. That Saturday morning, at the entrance to the cul-de-sac, she set up the lemonade stand and set out the lemonade that the girls had made the night before. Mama J's two older grandsons were put in charge. But after two hours Cecilia, Veronica and Mama J's grandsons only made three dollars and surrendered. The girls gave the leftover lemonade to the men who were cutting the yards. Their defeat was soon forgotten as they joined the rest of the kids in Lora's house who were blowing up balloons with all the air in their lungs that they could muster, and making Mother's Day cards. The kids banned Lora from the house because they had something special to do—a surprise. So Lora went to Edna's and helped peel and cut up the potatoes for potato salad. While she was gone, the girls and Mama J's grands made a Happy Mother's Day sign and practiced their speeches.

The neighborhood retired early that night—exhausted from the tasks, and resting up for tomorrow's big day. Lora was waiting up for Frank's call, which he always made promptly at 10 o'clock every night. When he called, she told him about the party and said, "I really want you to come. It'll be a great time for you to meet my neighbors. And, after all, it is a special day for me—Mother Day." He declined, saying that he had a business commitment.

She responded by saying, "But I thought Sunday was our day to be together, that you would be available?"

"Are you questioning me, Lora? Do you think I am lying?"

"No, I'm just disappointed," she replied.

The morning of the big event, as the girls and Mama J headed to church, Lora assured them she would take care of setting up the decorations and everything would be ready for the party when they returned from church. No matter the occasion, Mama J never missed church—a lesson she taught the girls that day.

After they left, Lora went over to Edna's and could smell the aroma of the marinated meat that Edna had just taken out of the fridge. Edna said she, Walter and Danny would not be going to church that morning because they needed to prepare for the party. "The Lord will understand if I miss a day, but don't tell Mama J I told you that," she said humorously to Lora.

Then Lora went over to talk with Big Lucy and Milky. They would be going to the late evening service at their church, Big Lucy explained. She and Milky started setting up the tables and chairs in the cul-de-sac, as well as the sound system. Milky said he would be the DJ, and started showing out, holding the microphone and shaking his shoulders and wiggling his hips, until Big Lucy told him to cut it out.

Lora went back to her house to gather and set up the decorations. "Why in the world did I not get the kids to do this?" she criticized herself as she had the tedious task of tying string to each of the balloons. She checked the girls' room and saw the Happy Mother's Day sign that the kids had made, and wondered where she should hang it. "Decisions, decisions," she said to herself as she could not think of where in the world to hang the sign. So she put it aside and went to hang the balloons. She tied a bunch of six to each of the mailboxes.

As she was doing this, she realized that Mr. Felix had not been invited. While they had never really introduced themselves, other than a friendly wave, she decided to take this opportunity to introduce herself and invite him to the party. She was surprised by how friendly he was, and quite a fit man for his age—he had a Jack Lalanne body and what appeared to be his real teeth. What was more of a surprise was that he said he would love to come, and asked if he could bring anything, or help with anything.

"Would you by any chance have any sorrel?" she asked. It was a Jamaican punch that Joseph had introduced to her, which she found delicious. Of course, she only drank the non-alcoholic version, without any rum or wine in it.

"Girl, what you know about sorrel?" he asked in his heavy Jamaican accent.

"Me been to Jamaica," she said, matching his accent, causing him to laugh and show all his perfect teeth.

She went back home and inflated six more balloons to hang on Mr. Felix's mailbox. She then went outside and laid out the tablecloths on the eight rectangular tables that were now set up. Walter set out in his yard his and Milky's grills, and the ribs were over the flames, and the smell of barbecue began now permeating the neighborhood.

Mama J's family began to pour in. They made their way into her house with bags of chips and desserts, and put them in serving bowls and trays that Mama had left out for the party tables. Lora looked at her watch, which read almost 2. Mama J and the girls were due home shortly. Lora rushed into the house to get dressed. She decided to wear a pair of orange and white striped Bermuda shorts and a sleeveless fitted orange knit top that accentuated her curves. "Tastefully sexy," she said to herself as she thought regretfully about Frank not coming to the party. Mama J and the girls arrived from church shortly before 2:30 and changed from their church clothes to comfortable clothes.

Milky turned on the sound system and opened the party by playing *ABC* by The Jackson Five as the middle of the cul-de-sac became populated with everyone dancing and loading up their plates with food.

While Mama J was eating and enjoying the kids dancing, Mr. Felix tapped her on the shoulder from behind and said "Happy Mother's Day, Mrs. Johnson. May I sit next to you?" as he handed her a bouquet of red roses. Mama J almost choked on her barbecue rib, but gestured to him *yes* and mumbled, "Suit yourself."

Happy Go Lucky felt like it was his party, as everyone was giving him their rib bones. Lora wondered if he could get sick from eating so much and made a mental note to ask the vet if there was anything like Pepto-Bismol for dogs.

"Attention, attention," Milky said on the microphone. "We now have a special presentation for all the mothers in the house." The kids came out carrying the sign that they had made, which Lora had not figured where best to hang it. Mama J's oldest grandson started out the presentation as Milky handed him the microphone.

"We want to thank all our mothers and Grandma for all that you do for us. Even though we might be bad sometimes, or not clean our room when you tell us, know that we always love you. Happy Mother's Day." The other kids read accolades from their note cards.

The girls were the last to speak. "Now we have a special poem by Cecilia and Veronica," Milky announced and handed the microphone to the girls.

"This poem is to all mommies who do not have a husband," Cecilia said as Veronica joined her to read the poem. It was a poem they had written with the help of Danny. Cecilia and Veronica alternated in reading each line.

Mothers are said to be the homemaker,
And fathers the provider.
But a woman who fulfills both roles,
No one can deny her.
What you earn you spend with control,
Making sure we aren't left in the cold.
You make sure we look perfect,
Before you look at your face,
Only because you love us,
A love that time cannot erase.
We say this because we love you,
And you love me,
And me,
A love that will last for all eternity.

While everyone was now clapping and the ladies wiping happy mist from their eyes, the kids handed out the cards to their mothers and Mama J. Cecilia and Veronica made Big Lucy a card as well, saying *Thank you for being a mother to the homeless people.*

Milky turned on the music and got the crowd back into a dancing mood. "Now this song is for the mothers in the house." While *We Are Family* by Sister Sledge played, Walter grabbed Edna's hand and swooped her up to dance. Milky did the same with Big Lucy. Mr. Felix bent down, extended his hand to Mama J, and asked, "May I please have the pleasure?" and she accepted. Danny asked Lora to dance with him. Mama J's daughters and husbands joined in, as did the kids.

It was now half past six, and time to wind down the party. All the ladies pitched in to clean up while the men took down the tables, folded up the chairs and put them in Milky's garage. Danny had the laborious task of cleaning the grills. Edna and Big Lucy made doggie bags for Mama J's family to take home. While the adults and Danny were engaged with the breakdown and cleanup, Lora supervised the kids who were having a last minute jumping contest on the trampoline. She thought she saw a shadow on the far side of her yard by the bushes, and figured it was Happy Go Lucky relieving his overstuffed stomach. Everyone exchanged hugs, thank you and goodbyes.

Lora was exhausted, but so pleased with how well things went, and was still overwhelmed with pride by the girls' poem. While she prepared for bed, she wondered if Frank would call that night at 10 as he usually did. Tired from the activities of the day, she dozed off, but at ten she was awakened by a ringing. It wasn't the telephone, however. Frank was at the door.

Frank explained that he felt so bad that he was not able to attend the party. But that he had to meet with this client who came from out of town, that it was a million-dollar contract.

"Lora, I am so sorry. You are such a good mother. I should have been with you today. But I'm glad you could be with your neighbors. This is for the best mother in the world. Happy Mother's Day." He handed her his gift—a pair of diamond studded earrings. "Lora, you are making me fall madly in love with you. But I don't know if that is what you want."

They consummated their relationship that night with a passion that that Frank had never experienced with any other woman.

"Frank, Frank, wake up. You have to leave. The girls will be awake soon."

◆ ◆ ◆

There had been concerns that Lora had wanted to discuss with Frank before their relationship was consummated—which she now had to address immediately. During their ten o'clock phone call the next night, she told Frank that they needed to talk as soon as possible, and asked if he could come over the following evening. Frank quipped, "Was it that good? You want an encore? That will absolutely be no problem." While this put levity into the conversation, it did not waive the seriousness of why Lora needed to talk with him. "We'll talk tomorrow, Frank. Goodnight." After they hung up, Frank thought to himself, "I hope she doesn't disappoint me. Commitment, a rose garden. Or maybe she is a gold digger? Now that would be surprising."

Frank arrived the next evening, shortly after the girls retired. He could tell it was not going to be an encore, as Lora answered the door in her work clothes and led him to the living room, where she took a seat in the Queen Chair and gestured for Frank to sit on the sofa. She offered him something to drink, but he declined, knowing that she did not have alcohol spirits—except that bottle of wine in her china cabinet that she said she was saving for a special occasion. "Frank, we need to talk, seriously." Lora was not going to put off the conversation any longer. Frank tuned in with his discerning ear, ready to listen, but hoping that it would not be one where he would have to drop her like a hot potato.

Lora's first concern was that now that they were being intimate, they needed to practice safe sex to prevent pregnancy and sexually transmitted diseases. Frank was not worried about this because he was sterile, and not being intimate with other women. He revealed this to Lora. Lora said she believed him, but wanted to see proof that he was sterile, which he said was no problem.

She also asked that he take an AIDS test. To this he took exception, as he said it was a gay man's disease, and he was certainly not gay, that he did not have any "sugar in his tank," and that he was offended. Lora explained to him that anyone can get the disease, and it could lie dormant for years. Without telling him why or when, she told him that she had taken an AIDS test and could show him that she was clean, and that he should show her the same. Frank's discerning ear was telling him he should be glad he was dealing with a woman who was concerned about safe sex. He agreed that he would take the AIDS test and show her the results.

Nonetheless, she continued, because they did not have an exclusive relationship, they should practice safe sex and he needed to wear a condom. Frank responded, "Well, why don't we make our relationship exclusive? Lora, I want you to be my woman, and I want to be your man—a monogamous relationship. What do you say?"

"Bring me those papers," she said seriously, "and I might say yes," she teasingly added. "I also need to know what you expect of me as your woman, and what I can expect from you as my man."

"I can show you one thing that I can give you right now," Frank said as he stood, took her hand and tried to lead her to the bedroom.

Lora was amused, and tempted, but she broke his embrace and redirected him to the front door. "It's late and I have to go to work tomorrow. Goodnight, Frank."

As Frank headed to his Augusta apartment, he thought about what he wanted from Lora. He knew that he wanted her to be exclusive to him, but there was more he wanted from her, though he just could not figure out what it was. And what did she expect of him? He could be exclusive to her—no more gold diggers—but if she wanted marriage, or him to be a father to those girls, well, he was not that man.

◆ ◆ ◆

All that week, the ladies talked about the Mother's Day block party and how wonderful it was. Mama J got teased to no end by Edna and Big Lucy.

"Girl, he put some wiggle in those hips," Edna teased as she slapped Mama J on her butt.

"Yeah, Mama J, don't fight the feeling. You know the Lord blessed old Sarah—having a baby at 90," Big Lucy said, cracking up herself and Edna with laughter.

Mama J just sat there trying to look stoic and dignified, while wanting to laugh out loud herself, and knowing too that she was impressed with Felix that day.

Lora framed the girls' poem and hung it on the wall next to their picture in the living room. She also had the photos developed that she had taken during the party and bought a photo album book. She gave the photos to the girls who put them in the album then ran to the neighbors, sharing the album with them.

While Danny had enjoyed the party, one thing perplexed him. He had seen Frank hiding in the bushes surreptitiously watching the party. Because he recognized the man as Lora's suitor, he did not become alarmed or say anything. But he felt it strange.

Frank had lied to Lora. He did not have a business appointment—he just didn't want to attend the party. Then he had a change of heart, and decided to attend after all. There was no place to park, so he left his car about a block away and walked over. However, as he approached the cul-de-sac he saw that there were so many people, loud music and kids running all over. He walked back to the opposite end of the cul-de-sac and found an entry into the back of Lora's yard. He hid behind bushes and watched the activities. He saw Lora dancing with Danny and yearned for her. Finally, he sneaked away, hoping that no one saw him.

◆ ◆ ◆

Looking for a commitment, and to continue to be intimate with Lora, Frank went to his private doctor that week and got an AIDS test, and a copy of his fertility report. He also asked the doctor to clarify what Lora told him about AIDS—being dormant and the risks of anyone getting it. The doctor confirmed the matter.

Lora and Frank met the following Sunday, while the girls were at church with Mama J, and picked up on their last conversation regarding their expectations from one another.

Frank was relieved that she was not looking for a marriage commitment, surrogate daddy for her girls or financial support. Lora's only requests were that their relationship be monogamous and that he respect the time that she needed to give to her girls.

"And what do you expect from me, Frank?" she asked.

"Lora, I expect nothing of you other than for you to be just the way you are. He pulled out a cassette from his jacket and asked her to put it on. As the song began to play, he took her in his arms, and as they slowly danced to the music, he softly sang along with Billy Joel while looking into her eyes…

I don't want clever conversation
I never want to work that hard
I just want someone that I can talk to
I want you just the way you are

After the song was over he told Lora he had to go, knowing that her girls would be coming home soon. He handed her the envelope containing his AIDS test and fertility clarification. "These are the documents you requested. I also bought this, in case you don't believe the documents," he said as he handed her a bag. He gave her a kiss and led himself to and out the door, as Lora stood there holding the envelope and bag.

Lora took the cassette player back to her bedroom and re-played the song, listening to the lyrics.

She opened the envelope, read the documents, and smiled. Then she opened the bag, saw the condoms and laughed.

Frank called Lora that night promptly at 10. Lora agreed she would be his woman, and he agreed he would be her man. After some sweet talk, Lora told Frank about some of her other concerns.

"Frank, as I told you, I want to keep our relationship discreet with people at my job. But if you are going to be part of my life, I need to explain to the girls. And I want you to meet my neighbors."

"Lora, don't make it sound so complicated. Tell the girls whatever makes you feel comfortable, and I'll meet your neighbors whenever you want."

Frank figured that maybe she should let the girls know about him, and then he could spend the night whenever he wanted. Maybe it would be good that he meets her neighbors. That way, they would stop looking at him so suspiciously when he came over. Also, they were good for babysitting. He had to be somewhat flexible, she wasn't asking for too much, he admitted to himself.

That week, one night as the girls were retiring, she told them that Frank was her special friend, and she liked him very much and hoped they would like him too.

"Why do you like him, Mommy?" they asked.

"Because he makes me happy and treats me special."

"But I thought we make you feel happy—and you are special."

"You can have more than one person in your life to make you feel happy and special. Just like you—you have not only me, but Happy Go Lucky, Mama J, Ms. Edna, Ms. Lucy, Danny. Name who else makes you happy."

"Patricia, Cedric and Johnny—he's so nice. Steve—he's so funny. Yeah, and Susan—she is pretty. What about Shanika—she is the smartest person in school, and—"

"Goodnight, ladies," Lora said as she turned off the light, leaving the girls to talk about all their friends.

The next Saturday, Lora invited Frank to meet the neighbors. It was yard day, and as the men were mowing the lawns, she took him to each house and introduced him to the men as they mowed, and to the ladies who were sitting on their front porches with lemonade to refresh the men. There were no long conversations—just a cordial exchange of "Nice to meet you." Lora knew Frank was out of his comfort zone, but she owed it to her neighbors to introduce them.

What bothered Frank was the whole scenario: the close proximity of the houses, the privacy—or lack thereof—of the cul-de-sac, all the neighbors being so close knit, and, most of all, Danny cutting Lora's lawn.

CHAPTER IX

Persuasions

Spring gave way to the summer, and Cecilia and Veronica were enjoying swimming and making friends at the new summer day camp. Danny, now 16 and having a car, stellar grades and excellent recommendations from his teachers, was able to get a full time summer job that paid him well above the $3.35 an hour minimum wage. Big Lucy and Milky were now helping build a new homeless shelter that was finally approved by the county legislators, thanks to their leadership and other community-concerned voices. Mama J and Mr. Felix were regularly waving to each other as they picked up the mail from their mailboxes each morning. And Lora went over the wish list she had made when fixing up the house.

The $5,000 from the insurance proceeds that she allotted for home improvements included painting of the exterior and a HVAC system. She also paid a visit to the pawnshop to get the vase out of hock—she only had one more month to buy it back. It cost her $600 to get it out of hock, yielding the pawnbroker a $200 profit. He asked Lora if she wanted to sell it for the $600, which she declined. She now was sure it was worth something and headed to an appraiser that her boss recommended. The appraiser said that she indeed had a valuable piece. The neoclassical French hand-painted porcelain vase was made around 1850, and worth around $3,500. The appraiser offered to sell it for a small commission. Lora declined. She wanted to keep it. "Never know when I might need it again, never know when hard times can hit," she thought to herself.

While Lora was enjoying her new air conditioning system, she was also enjoying more time with Frank. Since she said she would be his woman and told her girls he was her special friend, and had introduced him to her neighbors, Frank came over pretty much any time he wanted. But he still had to abide by her rule that he not interferes with the time she needed to be with the girls. That included tennis lessons on Saturday afternoon and homework and dinner time in the early evenings. And her rule that he could not spend the night also still stood—although he sometimes stayed until the wee hours of the morning.

He still could not persuade Lora to hire a babysitter, as she still was firm about only entrusting her neighbors to take care of the girls. So nights out were limited to once a month, which included dinner at a posh restaurant, jazz nightclubs, movie premiers and spending the night at his Augusta apartment.

Frank would often make impromptu visits to the house. Sometimes they would be when Lora was at work. He would go into her backyard and stay awhile. He would leave little tokens on the back patio, letting her know he'd been there—such as a basket of fruit or vase of flowers—and it always included a note that said, *I'm missing and watching you.* His tinted car windows allowed him to not have to acknowledge the ladies sitting in their porches. He thought for sure they were watching him.

And indeed they were. They noticed that Frank's visits were now as constant in the neighborhood as Jehovah's Witnesses. They were trusting of the JW's who believed in Jesus, but they were not trusting of Frank.

"Something about the way he walks, like a sneaky cat. But he is kinda cute. Almost as white as my Milky," Big Lucy observed.

"I think he's just a snob, uncomfortable in this neighborhood, a *bougie*. You see the kinda car he drives. But better that Lora got a man who has some money than one of those broke ass…. Oops, sorry Mama J," Edna said, catching her tongue.

"Ain't no church man, that's fo' sure," said Mama J as she leaned back in her patio chair.

"But what matters is that Lora and the girls are happy," all the ladies concurred.

Lora was happy for the most part in that Frank was attentive and always wanted to be with her. Nights that he was not with her, he would be sure to make his 10 o'clock call to say goodnight. And she felt that he loved her.

Although she was not looking for a father figure for her girls, Lora often thought how nice it would be if Frank took her and the girls to the zoo, aquarium, a trip to Magic Mountain or simply a day at the park with lunch at McDonald's. But she was not going to force Frank on the girls, or them on him.

There also were times that she felt Frank was being controlling, but she thought this was because he cared so much about her. Such an incident happened on one of Frank's impromptu visits.

While waiting for Lora to come home from playing tennis with the girls, he sat in his car in the driveway, watching Danny cut her yard. When she got home, Frank told her Danny did not need to cut her yard anymore. He said his company had professional landscapers who could do the job, and it would be no cost because he had a contract with them that was being underutilized. In fact, they were being paid for more work than he had properties available. Lora said she appreciated his offer, but must decline because this would be like firing Danny, and that he needed the money and liked his job. They did not see eye to eye, and it almost escalated to an argument. Later that evening, Lora felt that she had been unappreciative of Frank, that he had good intentions and wanted to do this because he cared. Nonetheless, she felt she made the right decision because of her relationship with Danny.

The next yard cut Saturday, Lora's lawnmower was not working. After having it checked by the mechanic, it was diagnosed that the motor blew because, somehow, the oil line had been severed. It would be best that she bought a new one rather than pay for the repairs. While she could afford to, the turn of events made her rethink Frank's offer. Lora knew that Danny now had a good paying summer job, and perhaps did not need the $10 dollars she was paying him. Then she thought that instead of Danny cutting the lawn, he could join her and the girls and play tennis with them on Saturdays. Lora presented this idea to Danny and told her about Frank's lawn service. Danny was quite pleased. He would no longer have to play tennis with his fence partner, and he always wanted to play tennis with Lora and the girls.

During their 10 o'clock call that night, Lora told Frank that she reconsidered his offer. Frank felt triumphant because the true reason why he did not want Danny to cut Lora's yard was because, since he was Lora's man, this should be his responsibility—not Danny's.

Frank's triumph was short lived, though, for he felt totally defeated when he found out that the time Danny was spending on Lora's yard was now being spent playing tennis with Lora and the girls.

He felt this was inappropriate. While Danny was now but only 16, he looked and acted like a man. Frank was jealous.

◆ ◆ ◆

Summer bid farewell to the fall, and fall to the winter as the neighborhood prepared for the festive holiday season. Frank told Lora that he would be spending Thanksgiving through Christmas in Chicago with his parents, but he would be back to spend New Year's Eve and Day with her.

"I wish you could come with me," he said deceitfully, knowing that if she came, she would have to bring the girls.

"Me too," Lora responded. She was being deceitful as well, knowing that she much preferred to spend the holidays with her neighbors and that the girls would be miserable if they had to spend so much time away from home in a place they did not know—or with Frank, for whom they felt no affection.

A couple of days before Thanksgiving, Frank came over to tell Lora goodbye for his flight, which departed that evening. He brought Christmas presents for her and the girls, and told Lora how much he was going to miss her. He assured her that he would call her as often as possible. But as Frank headed out and hit the highway, he did not go to the airport. Rather, he headed to his condominium in Atlanta.

That Christmas, the neighbors exchanged gifts, and Lora and the girls had Christmas dinner at Mama J's house with her children and grands. Danny *had* planned to get his car painted with the money he made that summer, but decided instead to use it to buy Christmas presents. He splurged by purchasing Edna and Walter a 32-inch color television for their bedroom. He also bought the girls their first bikes—a two-for-one sale at K-mart. For Lora, he bought a miniature crystal figurine of an angel. It was a coincidence that Lora also bought him a figurine of an angel to hang in his car.

Frank bought the girls some Barbie dolls, and Lora a sterling necklace with a small inscribed silver medallion that read, *You Belong to Me*. Lora bought Frank a hardback copy of Mahatma Gandhi's autobiography, a book that she was sure he had not read and hoping it would instill in him some compassion for the less fortunate.

Frank called that night, promptly at 10. He and Lora wished each other a Merry Christmas and expressed how much they missed each other. Lora told him that the girls liked his gifts, and she the necklace. "And how are your parents, Frank?" He replied that they were doing fine, and that he told them about her. He told her he would call her back tomorrow to discuss New Year's Eve plans.

However, Frank had not gone to Chicago, and he never had any intention to go. It was only a ruse because he didn't want to tell Lora the reason he did not want to be with her because he did want to be around her girls and neighbors. Instead, he chose to spend Christmas Eve at the strip joint *making it rain* by throwing up dollar bills, wondering which one of the gold diggers he would invite to his Atlanta condo. He didn't choose the prettiest or sexiest, but the one that he thought looked most vulnerable, innocent. She arrived at around 3:00 am after the strip joint closed. He answered the downstairs intercom and let her into the building. When she rang his doorbell, he handed her $100 and told her he had changed his mind. Frank had already satisfied himself thinking about Lora.

The next day, Lora, in anticipation of her and Frank spending New Year's together, asked Edna if the girls could stay overnight on New Year's Eve, knowing she and Walter stayed home on that night. Edna said it would be their pleasure. Frank called that night and gave Lora details. He wanted to take her to a party in Atlanta being hosted by one of his VIP business associates.

A couple of days later, Lora received FedEx packages from Saks Fifth Avenue and Neiman Marcus. In the Saks package she found a sequined midnight blue, fitted, short cocktail dress, and a silver fox fur shawl. In the Neiman package were a pair of matching satin three-inch pumps and a silver rhinestone clutch purse. Lora tried them on and looked into her full length mirror. She felt like Narcissus looking at his reflection in the water. "Wow! Wow! Wow!" she exclaimed, as she turned from side to side in the mirror. She read the price tags that were still on the garments—they more than quadrupled the cost, if not more, of all the clothes, shoes, purses and accessories in her wardrobe.

As Lora was taking off the clothes, she put on the song that Frank gave her.

Don't go trying some new fashion
Don't change the color of your hair
You always have my unspoken passion
I love you just the way you are.

Lora packed everything back into their original packages and wrote on the front *Return to Sender*. She let Frank know that she received the gifts and how lovely they were, but she did not tell him of her intent to return them.

Instead, that night she chose to wear the same dress and shoes she wore on their first date at the swanky restaurant. She did wear the diamond studded earring he gave her for Mothers' Day, and the necklace he gave her for Christmas with the inscription *You Belong to Me*. She knew it would be cold that night, so she splurged on a warm black wool coat that she bought from JCPenney.

Frank hired a limo that night. When he arrived, dressed in a black dinner jacket and bow tie, he was much surprised and highly disappointed that she was not wearing the outfit he bought. He didn't ask any questions, but his disappointment was obvious from his quiet disposition. Lora did not give any explanation, apology or try to force any conversation. They sat in silence for the first half hour of the nearly two-hour drive to Atlanta. Lora broke the silence by asking Frank if he could put on some music. He reached forward to turn on the radio and cassette player that was hooked up in the back. "What's your pleasure, Lora?" he asked as he tried to tune to a station. She opened her clutch purse and handed him the cassette. Without looking at the label, he put the cassette on to play.

Don't go trying some new fashion
Don't change the color of your hair
You always have my unspoken passion
I love you just the way you are.

He got the message, started to smile and turned to look at her. As he leaned toward her for a kiss, he noticed on her neck the necklace he bought her with the inscription *You Belong to Me*. For the rest of the ride, their hands and bodies were busy like two teenagers at a drive-in movie exploring forbidden fruit.

At the New Year's Eve party, even though she was not dressed in designer fashions like most of the ladies, Lora was comfortable with the way she looked—once she checked her JCPenney coat at the door. The crowd was lively, with many guests already intoxicated from drinks being replenished by the pretty young waitresses, and bartenders displaying their skills by shaking canisters, pouring drinks and topping them with maraschino cherries, lime and olives. There was a wide variety of music from old school to new school. Lora was sitting back on one of the settees, watching people dance, while Frank made his way around the room schmoozing with his business associates. Frank had not introduced Lora to anyone. Lora thought perhaps this was because she did not dress the way he wanted her to. However, this thought was dismissed when Frank came over and whispered in her ear, "There is not one person in this room that I care about, except you. This is just all about business. We'll be out of here soon."

At the stroke of midnight, everyone grabbed someone to kiss, as did Frank, who gave Lora a kiss and said, "Let's get the hell out of here." He hurriedly led her out of the ballroom and hotel to the limousine parking lot and had the attendant page his driver. When they reached his Atlanta 20-floor condo complex, he told the driver it was their final destination, thanked him and gave him a generous tip.

It was Lora's first time to visit Frank's Atlanta residence. It was quite different from his modest Augusta apartment. While it was immaculately clean, had state-of-the-art appliances and expensive modern furniture, it felt uninhabited. This was because Frank rarely stayed there. He usually used the condo for business meetings, and where his out of town business guests would stay. The only room that Frank made inviting was the master bedroom. This was because it was where he would woo the gold diggers and clinging vines before he met Lora.

The vaulted ceiling, cream-colored room was tastefully and warmly furnished with a king sized bed, covered with a plush dark burgundy bedspread and matching oversized decorative floral pillows. The bed faced an entertainment center that included a 50-inch television, stereo and speakers. Vases with an assortment of flowers and framed abstract art prints accentuated the room.

Frank had never seen Lora in lingerie, so he bought her a lavender silk lace ensemble for this occasion. He gave it to her in a gift bag as she headed to the master bathroom to prepare for the night. While she was in the bathroom, Frank turned on some soft jazz, dimmed the lights and prepared a tray with a bottle of champagne, glasses and chocolate covered strawberries. Although alcohol had never touched Lora's lips, Frank hoped that tonight he would take this virginity.

While Lora was in the bathroom, she thought about the party and the intoxicated guests. She had not been to a party since the Jamaican house parties that she and Joseph went to—but these people would get intoxicated by the fun, the laughter and the music rather than alcohol. She thought about this place—Frank's home. Other than the bedroom, she thought how she could make it look so cozy and warm—just like she had transformed Joseph's place. She looked at the lingerie and thought how much more comfortable her oversized cotton t-shirt would feel. When Lora exited the bathroom in the lavender lingerie, Frank felt his $150 had been well spent.

As they lay in bed, Frank put one of the chocolate covered strawberries in Lora mouth, and then poured her a glass of champagne. While she gladly accepted the strawberry, she refused the champagne. So he drank it as she reached for another strawberry. After she ate another three strawberries, and he drank another glass of champagne, he asked her why she did not drink. She shared with him something that she had not shared with anyone except Joseph—not even Mama J. Her biological mother had been an alcoholic and drug addict. She died when Lora was three.

Frank poured himself another glass of champagne. He then asked her why, since she was no longer married, she did not go back to her maiden name. She asked him why should she? He said he thought she should since that man was no longer a part of her life. She said that she disagreed; because she had children by him who were named Jones, she should keep the name.

"Is there any way I can persuade you, Lora? I don't like you having the name of another man," Frank persisted.

"Even if I did," she replied, "my name would still be Jones, because Jones is my maiden name."

"I'll be damned," Frank muttered as he took the last gulp of his fourth glass of champagne. "Well, why don't I change that by making you Mrs. Parker?"

Lora knew that he was tipsy from the champagne, and that this was pillow talk. "Frank, I think you've had enough of that champagne," she replied, as he clicked off the light and took her in his arms.

◆ ◆ ◆

There had been times when Lora had thought about remarrying, and when she did, Joseph's last words echoed in her mind, "Make sure you truly know him."

But more important to Lora was that the person who she married must love her children. She knew that Frank did not love the girls, and that he was doing nothing to really gain their affection. Also, she was aware that the girls were not comfortable with him. She recalled one afternoon, after telling the girls that Frank was coming over, when she heard them from their bedroom:

"Knock, knock."

"Who's there?"

"Frank."

"Frank who?"

"Frankenstein."

Lora thought that if the girls truly understood the story of Frankenstein, they would realize Frankenstein—who they thought was a monster—was not. Rather, it was something that needed to be loved, to be understood—just like Frank.

CHAPTER X

Decisions

DANNY WOULD BE GRADUATING FROM HIGH school that year, and the mailbox at the Ayoka's address was overstuffed every week with college information—colleges that he had applied to as well as those recruiting students of his caliber. His 3.95 GPA, 1390 SAT score and recommendations from teachers made him a desirable candidate. While he was not sure what he wanted to major in, he was absolutely sure that he wanted that "paper chase"—a college diploma. He wanted it not only for himself, but for his parents. The education would be his, but the diploma would belong to them. He would have it framed and present it to them to hang on their wall.

Because they had never had the opportunity to attend college, this was a time that was paramount in the life of Walter and Edna. Edna had worked as a nursing aide until she was 40, when she gave birth to Danny. Walter started his working career at minimum wage as a stock person and worked his way up to stocking supervisor at a major retail store. What earned him the respect of the company and his co-workers was his work ethic and how he interacted with others—quiet, kind, humble, yet decisive and clearly one that others could not push around. He knew about every facet of the retail business, from the service desk to the managerial duties to the executive duties. The only thing that stopped him from getting a higher position was that he did not have a college degree.

Edna's hope for her son's future was to get a college education, a good paying job, marry a Christian woman and provide her with grandchildren.

Walter's ambition for Danny was more demanding. He wanted Danny to be a man that would influence others, to be financially independent and to make a difference in the world. He wanted Danny to find a career that he felt passionate about, rather than one that he only worked at to make money. He wanted him to marry a woman, like his Edna, who would be his soul mate. He wanted him to be a kind and loving father and spend time with his children no matter how busy his career.

The letters from the colleges that Danny had applied to all read *Congratulations, you have been accepted....* There were two Ivy League schools, four schools with full scholarships, and several others that he had not applied to but that were still trying to recruit him with offers of enticing scholarships. It was now time to make a decision.

"You know which school I want you to choose," Edna said with certainty.

"Son, ultimately it's your choice, but I agree with your mother," said Walter. "While it would be costly, and the other schools are offering full scholarships, in the long run, going to this school will open doors for you that none of the other schools are going to do. Your mother and I will find a way to cover the cost. Once you finish, you will be in a situation to give back to us, and we will be proud parents that our son went to such a fine institution."

So Danny accepted the offer to attend Harvard University. However, he was worried about the financial burden it would put on his parents. But he felt that nothing could outweigh how proud they would be if he attended Harvard.

Edna was on the phone the next day calling her sister Erma, two years her senior, and everyone else she knew to tell them the good news. And the normally quiet and humble Walter bragged to his co-workers the next day.

Mama J, Big Lucy and Lora all said it called for a celebration. "Another block party!" they exclaimed. Lora also had something in mind that she wanted to do for Danny.

"I'm taking the girls to Disney World on spring break, and I would like to treat Danny as well—a graduation present. What do you think, ladies?" They thought it was a great idea. Mama J's grandkids went to Disney World a couple of years ago and could not stop talking about how much fun they had. She had a Mickey Mouse hat and other souvenirs that they brought back for her. One year, Milky and Big Lucy helped raise money to send a group of the homeless kids to Disney World, and they all had a great time as well.

Lora and the ladies presented their ideas to Edna and Walter—Disney World trip in the spring, and a graduation party—a block party--that summer. With the permission of the proud parents, the ladies started their planning.

Lora thought that perhaps Walter and Edna might want to go on the Disney trip too. Walter said it would be impossible because he would be busy at the store with spring inventory, but Edna said she would love to go.

Spring break was only two weeks away, so Lora called a travel agency and booked a three-day weekend group package, and hotel rooms. Danny would have his own room, and Edna, Lora and the girls would share a double sized room. Lora had planned to take her station wagon, but Walter insisted that they take the Cadillac because it was new and they would not have to worry about any car problems. He also felt that they would be more comfortable with the plush, roomy seats, headrests, stereo and the quiet air conditioning. Perhaps, however, the most important reason—which he kept to himself—was that Danny would feel so good driving his brand new Cadillac.

Danny jumped with joy when Edna told him about the trip after he got home from his part-time job. He was delighted to be able to spend this time with Cecilia and Veronica, and thought about how much fun it was going to be to take them on the many rides. He also pictured himself cruising on the highway in Walter's car—king of the road. He had always wanted to go to Disney World.

"It was Lora's idea—a graduation gift from her to you," Edna said, as she handed him the brochures Lora had given to her. Danny went to his room, took a quick shower, changed into a fresh t-shirt and jeans and went to Lora's house to thank her. He wondered what he would say to her just as he started to feel that that quivering sensation in his stomach.

Lora had just said goodnight to the girls as Danny rang the doorbell. "Danny, so good to see you. Come on in."

"No, thank you. I have to get back and study for a test tomorrow, but I wanted to come over and thank you for the graduation gift—the trip to Disney World."

"Are you sure you want to come with us? I was thinking maybe you would prefer to go with some people your age?"

"On no, I much prefer being with the girls. They're so special to me."

"Well, that's just how they feel about you. Do you know that one day they asked me if they could call you Uncle Danny?"

"Really?" Danny replied, smiling from ear to ear.

Just as Lora was about to tell Danny more, Frank pulled into the driveway. "I need to go now, Mrs. Jones. Thank you again, and I look forward to the trip." As Danny headed back to his house, Frank climbed out of the car, and Danny gave him a courteous nod.

"Why was he here?" Frank asked, perturbed.

"I'll tell you all about it," she said as she gave him a hug and kiss. "But first tell me about your day?" she asked, as she led him to the dining room and poured a glass of Jack Daniels for him from a bottle that he brought over.

"My day was inconsequential, Lora. Just tell me why that boy was here." He finished the whiskey with one gulp.

Lora went on to tell Frank about the trip—how much the girls were looking forward to it, that it would be a graduation present for Danny, and he could help her with the six-hour drive. She started telling him that she booked hotel rooms, but before she could tell him that Edna was going also, Frank exploded with anger. While he refrained from raising his voice so that the girls could not hear, the rage in his voice and fury in his face frightened Lora.

"Are you crazy? You're going to take a weekend trip and stay at a hotel with that big black Mandingo! Do you know what boys do at his age—they masturbate all the time because all they can think about is sex! He already plays tennis with you every Saturday, and I bet you he's over there every night jerking off while thinking about you. Maybe you're already sleeping with him. Is that the case? Is it, Lora?" At this point, Frank was clenching Lora by her forearms so forcefully that she winced with pain, and pleaded with him to stop, that he was hurting her. Lora was then speechless, shocked by Frank's absurd allegations, still feeling the pain in her arms. "I'm out of here. If you want me in your life, Lora, I don't want that boy anywhere around you!" Frank exclaimed as he headed out, slammed the door, jumped in his car, floored the accelerator and sped away.

Lora had not heard from Frank for a week, and tried to break the silence by writing and mailing to him a letter.

Dear Frank,

It saddens me that you have so little faith and trust in me that you could make such accusations. I am equally disappointed that you do not have enough confidence in yourself—that you are jealous of a young man who is no threat to you. You once told me that you were falling in love with me, but you never told me that you actually love me. Nor have I told you that I love you. Well, I am telling you that now—I do love you. And for that reason, you should not be jealous.

You have given me the ultimatum that if you are to be in my life, Danny cannot be part of mine. To me this choice is not a choice between you and Danny, rather it is a choice of whether or not I want to be in a relationship with you wherein you do not trust me and believe that I am devoted to you.

You have never wanted to partake in activities with the girls. Danny has been like a big brother to them. I invited him on the trip so that he could spend time with them, something you would never do. If you are jealous of that, it is of your own devising—I haven't given you any reason for it.

Also, to relieve your warped imagination, you should know that Danny's mother will be accompanying us on the trip. You would have known this if you had been more patient and open.

So, what I am trying to say to you is that I love you and want to be with you, but not if you don't trust me or respect my judgment.

Lora

◆ ◆ ◆

The evening before the trip, Walter and Danny took the Cadillac to the service station, filled it up with gas, checked the fluids and pressure in the tires and made sure the spare in the trunk had air. Edna prepared snacks—finger sandwiches, cut up fruits and vegetables, cookies, chips—and packed a cooler with water and beverages. Lora packed comfortable clothes and toiletries, and she purchased some games that the girls could play in the car. She also packed the girls' pillows, paper towels and a can of deodorizer for those "stinkies"—farts.

That morning, before leaving for work, Walter exchanged car keys with Danny. He reiterated driving instructions and precautions, and reminded Danny to make sure he called him and let him know when he arrived, and to take care of his mother, Lora and the girls.

At 9:00 am sharp, Danny loaded up the car. The girls were forcing themselves to pee as Lora told them that it would be six hours before they got to a bathroom. Lora and Edna made last minute checks to make sure they had not forgotten anything. As they locked up their houses, Mama J and Big Lucy came out to wish them a safe and fun trip. Cecilia and Veronica were busy saying goodbye to Happy Go Lucky and Mama J promised she would take good care of him while they were gone.

"Is everyone buckled up?" Danny asked as he pressed the accelerator, and headed out with everyone waving goodbye, and Happy Go Lucky wagging his tail.

Lora had hoped she would hear from Frank before she left, but she was not going to let it spoil the trip. Perhaps this time away from each other would help them both think more clearly, she hoped.

Frank purposefully hadn't contacted Lora before the trip because he was still hoping she would cancel. He called her that night, and because she did not answer, he knew that she had left. Lora's letter to him, professing her love for him was not enough for his ego. He felt that the only way he could trust her was for her to be completely compliant to whatever he requested. It was enough for him to be accepting of her children, something that he could do nothing about. Consumed with anger, he wanted to walk away from the relationship. He went to the strip joint that weekend, made it rain once again and this time the gold digger did spend the night, and another one the next night, and the next night. But all he could think about was Lora and the cringing thought of her being with Danny.

Cecilia and Veronica, as well as Danny, were having the time of their lives as they enjoyed the rides and explored the theme parks. Edna could not keep up with the pace, so she and Lora spent their time on the tour buses, shopping for souvenirs, and an afternoon at the spa getting a massage, manicure and pedicure. As Edna and Lora were getting their mani and pedi, Lora asked Edna how she and Walter met.

"Marriages in our village were arranged by families. The boy's family had to give the girl's family goats in exchange for their daughter's hand, a dowry. My parents had picked out two boys of their likin' for me to marry. They choose Abah, a boy whose family had more goats than Walter's family. But Abah did not like me, nor did I like him, not in the marriage sense. He said to me that if he had to marry me, he would kill himself, because he did not like girls. But Walter and I were crazy about each other, and Abah was our friend. So Walter and Abah came up with a plan. They killed four of Abah's family goats. They felt bad about killing them, but also knew that it would be good eating for the whole village. And Walter's parents now had the most goats, so we got married. When we look back on it now, we realize that if it had ever been discovered, Walter would have been stoned to death, and that Abah would have had his genitals cut off for being gay. That's why, even though most people think homosexuality goes against Christian beliefs, me and Walter don't think so. Abah was one on the most Christian-like persons we had ever known."

Lora made a mental note that perhaps someday she could talk to Walter and Edna about Joseph.

◆ ◆ ◆

"One more picture, everyone, before we head home," Danny called out. Edna took the last picture as the girls stood on each side of Lora and Danny stood behind them extending the full length of his wing span, a distance that could only be matched by the smile on his face.

CHAPTER XI

Consequences

HAPPY GO LUCKY STARTED YELPING, WAGGING his tail, jumping up and scratching on Mama J's door as soon as the Cadillac pulled up and its glad-to-be-home passengers exited the car. Mama J turned down the fire on her black-eyed peas and hurried to open the door. Happy Go Lucky could not get enough of the girls' hugs as he licked them like a lollipop. While Danny was lugging everything out of the car, Lora and Edna started talking to Mama J about the trip until she interrupted them and advised, "Y'all should get some rest, 'specially you, Edna. You look kinda tired…but your feet sho' look nice," she said as she noticed Edna's red painted toenails in the flip flops that she bought at Disney World. Everyone proceeded to their house, and was glad for Mama J's advice as they enjoyed the comfort of their own beds that night.

"Walter, I really missed you," Edna said. "Although it was only three days, this was the longest time we have ever been apart."

"I missed you too," Walter said as he turned off the light and held her close to him.

That week, the talk was about the Disney trip. Lora had the 12 rolls of film developed and made copies for both she and Edna, and showed the photos to Mama J and Big Lucy. Danny had bought a t-shirt for Walter. On the front it read *I Love Disney World,* and on the back, *But I Love My Dad More.* Lora bought Mama J a pair of Mickey Mouse slippers, Milky a Mickey Mouse t-shirt and Big Lucy a matching Minnie Mouse t-shirt. The girls bought everyone, including Mr. Felix and their school friends, little trinkets. Danny also bought a souvenir for himself—a bumper sticker for his car that read *I left my heart in Disney World.*

It was the weekend before Spring Break would end. Lora planted the last of the annual flowers that she had bought. It always bothered her that these beautiful flowers had such a short lifespan. As she was planting them, she thought of Frank. As much as she wanted to call him, she refrained. If he was not going to respond to the letter she sent to him, it meant that he really didn't care. She would put this relationship behind her and not let it hurt. She did this with her relationship with her adoptive parents and her relationship with Joseph, too, which were far longer and deeper than the relationship she had with Frank. She felt that no matter how much you love someone, you cannot force them to love you. Holding on to someone who doesn't want you will eventually make them resent you, or you them, or both.

Before long school was back in session, and Lora was due back at the nursery. She was late that morning because of an accident that stopped traffic at the highway. She apologized to her boss for being late and he noted that others were also late because of the accident.

"It looked to be a bad one, and this is going to delay our shipments that are due today. So, I was wondering if you could work late this evening?" he asked Lora.

Rarely had her boss asked her to work overtime because he knew she had to pick up the girls from school, but she felt obligated and said she would. Her plans were to pick up the girls after school, leave them with Edna, and then return to work. On her lunch break, she called Edna to see if she could watch the girls that evening, but there was no answer. She was confident, however, that Edna would.

"How was school today?" she asked the girls as they fumbled in the back of the car to put on their seatbelts. Lora only half listened as she thought about all the pruning that needed to be done at the nursery. She would have to work until 9 or so to get everything done. "Mommy has to work this evening, so you'll be staying at Ms. Edna's house until I get home," she told the girls.

After checking the mailbox and opening the door for the girls, Lora went over to Edna's house. Walter's Cadillac was there, but there was no answer as she rang the doorbell several times. So she went over to Mama J's, but still no answer. She then went over to Big Lucy's, and again there was no answer. She tried to call them, but only the answering machines came on. This was strange, thought Lora. While she was worried about who would watch the girls, she was now also worried about her neighbors. Where could they all possibly be? Then the doorbell rang.

It was Mr. Felix. He informed her that Walter had been in a car accident that morning, that all the neighbors were at the hospital's emergency ward. He did not tell her what condition Walter was in. As he was about to leave, Lora asked him, "Mr. Felix, can you watch the girls for me?" He told her that his niece was visiting him, that he would send her over to babysit. Lora called her boss and told him reluctantly that she could not work that evening because she had to go to the hospital, that she thinks it was her neighbor who was involved in the accident that morning. He told Lora not to worry, that he would do the pruning himself.

Mr. Felix's niece arrived. Lora introduced her to the girls, instructed her to give them the frozen dinners in the freezer, that they needed to do their homework, and at half past 7, they needed to prepare for bed. Just as Lora was about to get into her car and head out to the hospital, Milky's car pulled up with Mama J in the back seat.

As Big Lucy helped Mama J out of the car, Milky told Lora the bad news: "Walter is dead, Lora."

Mama J was too distraught to talk, as Big Lucy held on to her and led her home. Big Lucy fixed some tea and made a grilled cheese sandwich while Mama J changed into a nightdress and slippers. "I'll be okay, Lucy. You get on home and get some rest. We'll talk tomorrow," Mama J said as she got her Bible and sat in her rocker. Big Lucy brought her the tray with the tea and grilled cheese sandwich and advised her to try eating something. She gave Mama J a hug and kiss, and let her know that she, too, would be praying that night.

Lora followed Milky into his house and sat at the kitchen table. It still had potatoes that Big Lucy was peeling when she heard Edna screaming. Milky dumped the graying potatoes in the trash, sat down at the table and told Lora what happened.

Danny took the bus to school that morning because Walter was taking Danny's car to get an estimate on how much a new paint job would cost—something he wanted to do for Danny as a graduation present. As Walter entered the highway, the car went out of control and hit the embankment, causing it to flip over. Walter was crushed under the steering wheel. When the ambulance arrived, they said Walter had died on impact. A police officer came to the house to inform Edna. Big Lucy heard Edna screaming as the police officer tried to embrace her. She fell to the ground. Mama J heard the screaming as well. Both ran out to see what was happening. Big Lucy called Milky at work, and he rushed home. Edna composed herself to call Danny's school and say that he needed to come home, and that it was urgent. A counselor at the school drove Danny home. Mr. Felix heard and saw the commotion. Mama J told him that they were headed to the hospital, and asked him to tell Lora where they were when she got home. When Milky and Danny got home, they all headed out to the hospital in Milky's car, and the police officer escorted them with the siren on to clear traffic. Edna and Danny were still at the hospital. Big Lucy joined in the conversation after leaving Mama J.

"There is nothing we, as neighbors, can do tonight," advised Milky.

"Except pray," added Big Lucy.

Lora was beyond tears, as she felt numbness in every fiber of her body. Rather than go into her house, she went into her backyard and sat there in her patio chair. She felt so lonely. She wanted someone to talk to. Milky and Big Lucy had each other; Mama J had her Bible and faith in Jesus. Then she felt guilty for feeling sorry for herself as she thought about what Edna and Danny were going through. She knew she would not be able to sleep that night. She went into the house where the girls were eating the frozen dinners that Mr. Felix's niece had heated in the oven.

"I'm sorry, dear, but I did not get your name," she asked.

"Tasha, ma'am."

"Tasha, how late can you babysit?"

"My uncle said I could stay as late as you need me, ma'am."

"Well, can you please call him and tell him I'll need you to stay at least until midnight?" Lora asked, as she handed her the phone. After Tasha spoke with her uncle, and he approved, Lora headed to the nursery.

Her boss was surprised to see her as he was laboriously pruning the plants, something that he had not done since he hired Lora. Lora told him that her neighbor, her friend, was killed in the accident, and that there was nothing she could do. That perhaps coming to work would help get her mind off what had happened.

As Lora pruned the shrubs and florals, cutting the dead parts to give way for new growth, she thought about how fragile life was, how unpredictable, how tragic it is when the unexpected happens. She looked over at the annuals that she was not fond of because of their short lifespan. Her attitude about them changed as she thought about what they represented. They were predictable; to see them die was not tragic because they had lived their life expectancy. Whereas the shrubs that she was pruning were expected to live many years. It would be disappointing if they died, especially for the time that it took to cultivate them. She wanted to think about the annuals and shrubs rather than Edna not growing old with Walter, rather than Walter not seeing Danny graduate from Harvard, rather than Walter now being dead. It was too dreadful to think about.

Lora worked until almost midnight. Her boss finally insisted that she go home. He told Lora how much he appreciated her coming in under the circumstances, and told her to take off the next day or two to spend time with her neighbors. He also said that the nursery would donate flowers for the funeral arrangement.

◆ ◆ ◆

There were nearly 200 people at Walter's funeral—people from his church, his co-workers, his barbershop buddies. Edna's older sister, Erma, flew in from New Jersey. Several of Danny's teachers and schoolmates paid their respects. Walter and Edna had several relatives in Nigeria who were not able to attend because of passport and financial reasons, but Edna's sister did send a telegram to an aunt who spread the word in their village. There they had a memorial service for Walter and all the villagers attended.

One person did fly in from Nigeria—Walter's and Edna's childhood friend, Abah, who served as one of the pallbearers. Danny wrote Walter's eulogy. Its words were so profound that even the seasoned pastor, who read the eulogy, was overcome with emotion several times. Big Lucy, who the neighbors did not know could sing, brought everyone to tears when she sang "Amazing Grace" *a cappella*.

Edna purchased a cemetery plot that allowed her to be buried next to Walter when she died. She picked out a mahogany coffin with brass handles. Mama J thought it was bittersweet that the coffin was of the same mahogany wood and brass hardware as the front door that Edna had always wanted. Lora was disturbed by the resemblance.

The cemetery attendant handed the shovel to Edna who scooped up the first shovel of dirt, and poured it over the submerged coffin. The cemetery attendant then handed Danny the shovel to put in the next scoop of dirt before they customarily took over to apply the rest of the dirt. But Danny refused to give him back the shovel, and continued to shovel in the dirt until his father's grave was covered.

Edna's sister stayed with her for the next several weeks, helping Edna to make the decisions that she needed to make, as her life would be changed drastically with Walter's passing. Walter had a $50,000 insurance policy from his job. The house had a $35,000 mortgage, which she would pay off with the insurance proceeds. This left her with only $15,000. They still owed $12,000 on the Cadillac. The finance company agreed that Edna would not have to make any further payments with no penalties, provided they take possession of the vehicle. Edna agreed. Walter's funeral costs were $6,000, which Edna's church, friends and Walter's co-workers pooled together and paid. While Edna still had $15,000 and no mortgage, she still had monthly living costs and homeowner taxes and insurance to pay. This added up to about $700 a month, if she stayed on a tight budget. While she would no longer have a car payment, she had no car and would have to buy a used one, or one that she could afford. She would not be eligible for her or Walter's Social Security payments for another five years. There was also Danny's tuition and housing payments to Harvard that would start that fall.

Erma thought that it would be best that Edna come live with her and her husband in New Jersey. She was savvy when it came to real estate and advised Edna of her options. Edna could sell the house, take equity out on it or rent it out—all of which would net her a source of income. Also, because Danny would be leaving for college, Edna, at her age, should not be living alone with the demanding physical responsibility of being a homeowner. Edna was still concerned about how Danny's tuition to Harvard would be paid, which was approximately $20,000 a year.

CONSEQUENCES

Danny listened attentively as his mother and aunt discussed these matters, but he did not intervene, suggest, agree or disagree. He just listened. That week, he sought the advice of his school counselor, Mr. Clarence Edwards, who was the one who drove Danny home the day that Walter died, attended the funeral and had always taken an interest in Danny—his most prized pupil.

"I cannot put this burden on my mother. Either I find a way to pay this tuition on my own, or I do not attend. Also, I don't want my mother to be dependent on anyone, not even my aunt. I can get a job with my high school degree, and go to a local college part time so that I can help my mother with the bills. Being able to help my mother means more to me than some fancy degree," Danny explained.

Mr. Edwards was not going to dictate what he thought Danny should do. Rather, he was going to look into the options that Danny had based on what Danny wanted to do, which was to not burden his mother. "Let me look into some things, son, and I'll get back with you in a couple of days."

He called Danny into his office that following Friday. "I spoke with the financial aid director at Harvard. There are several financial aid packages you can apply for that will cover your tuition, books, housing and meals. However, once you graduate, you will be close to $100,000 in debt.

"There are several colleges in the local area, many of them very reputable, some that have already offered you scholarships. However, to be eligible for their scholarship packages, you must be a full-time student and maintain a B in all your classes. This means you will only be able to work part time unless you are superman and can stay awake 24/7.

"There is another option—the U.S. military. There is a special enlistment for those who qualify. You will be trained in a special force. Your training and service will be accredited to a college degree, including a Masters, in a related discipline. In addition, you will be paid a full salary that is higher than you can receive in a regular job as a high school graduate. They are highly selective, and only about two percent of those who apply are selected. The downside is that you have to enlist for 10 years. But once you enlist, your financial problems will be resolved. They also give you an allotment for your dependents. In your case, that would be your mother. Here are some brochures that you might want to look at."

Mr. Edwards further advised Danny that he needed to make a decision soon, as applications were time sensitive. He gave Danny his home telephone number, and said to call him any time. "Make sure you give your mother my regards."

"Thank you, Mr. Edwards, I really appreciate this," Danny said, as he shook the hand of his caring counselor. As Danny was about to leave, Mr. Edwards asked him to hold on a minute, and opened his desk drawer.

"Your classmates asked me to give this to you. Don't open it now. Open it when you get home." He handed Danny an envelope, which Danny figured was a sympathy card, and a small wrapped box. He did not want Danny to open the box in his presence because he did not want Danny to see him get emotional. Danny thanked him again and headed out to take the city bus home.

As Danny was riding home on the bus, he thought about the options that Mr. Edwards had presented to him. It was clear to him which one he wanted, but he was not sure how his mother would feel. Never in his life had he defied her—whatever she said was best. But in this case, he might have to go against her wishes. He had to be a man, and make decisions himself. He felt that his decision was what his father would want him to make—one that would best enable him to take care of his mother.

Danny was now at his stop and stepped off the bus. But before proceeding to walk the two blocks to his house, he sat down on the bus bench and opened the envelope. It was a sympathy card, as he had expected. But what he did not expect was all the people who signed it—the signatures covered the front, inside and back, and some even overlapped because there was not enough room to write. He then opened the box. It was a car key, the title to a car and the name of the person and the place where he would pick it up. Danny eyes became misty as he thought how kind this was of his classmates, Mr. Edwards. But as he held the key in his hand, he remembered how the key to his father's old car felt when his father put it in his hand; the car that his father was killed in while taking it to get painted for him. All the anguish that he been holding back to be strong for his mother, came pouring out as he sat on the bus bench and cried for nearly hour.

Late that evening Danny called Mr. Edwards, told him how much he appreciated the car. "But I might not need it, Mr. Edwards, because I have decided I want to enlist. I looked at the brochures and want to apply to be a medic in the U.S. Marines."

"I think you've made a wise decision, Danny. I have a personal friend who works in the recruitment office. I will call him this weekend, and see if he can meet with you Monday. I suggest that you speak with your mother about this before you make a final decision."

"Of course. I am going to talk with her tomorrow. If I'm accepted, I won't need the car, but would it be okay if I gave it to my mother?" Mr. Edwards assured him that it would be more than okay.

Edna's sister was up early. Danny was awakened by the smell of the sizzling bacon. He joined his Aunt Erma in the kitchen, whipped up some batter and made some pancakes as she scrambled eggs. Edna, who did not want to get out of bed, could not resist the smell of the bacon, got up as well and made some coffee. As they were eating, they heard the lawnmowers cranking up, and Edna and Danny realized it was lawn cutting day. They both looked at each other sadly, remembering that this was Walter's job—one that he liked doing and took pride in how his lawn looked. Danny immediately got up, excused himself and went out to cut the yard. But when he opened the door, Mr. Felix was already there.

"Me got it, mon!" Mr. Felix called out.

Danny rejoined his mother and aunt at the table and told them of Mr. Felix's kind deed. There were a few pieces of bacon and a couple spoonful of eggs left on the stove that Danny spooned onto his plate. His aunt complimented Edna on how nice her neighbors were.

"Yes, I'm really going to miss them," Edna said sadly.

"What, mama?" asked Danny confused.

His aunt went on to explain. "Your mother and I decided that she should move to New Jersey with me when you graduate this June. The house is going to be put up for rent for two years. This will give your mother time to think about what she really wants to do, and bring in some income while she is trying to decide. With what is left over from the insurance policy, the rent and a little contribution from me, it'll be enough to pay tuition for at least a year of your tuition at Harvard. After that, we'll just take it one day at a time, and rely on the Lord to make a way."

Danny felt that this was an opportune time to reveal to his mother his decision. He gave his mother and aunt the details as Mr. Edwards explained to him, and what made him make the decision. "When I am finished, I will have the training and credentials to go to Harvard Medical School and become a doctor—a medical doctor. And, Mama, you won't have to worry about finances—my college education will be completely paid for, plus I'll be able to send you money."

"I like that, Danny. Your father will be so proud," Edna said as she broke down in tears. Erma comforted her sister and suggested that she go back to bed and get some more rest. Danny realized too that his mother needed it—she has been through too much.

While his aunt was putting his mother to bed, Danny cleaned up the kitchen, as worry consumed him. "Will they accept me? Will I qualify to be a medic?" After cleaning up the kitchen, he went into the family room and looked at the worn recliner where Walter would sit and watch sports. He then went into the backyard and looked at the basketball court that Walter built.

"Is this what my father wants me to do?" He picked up the basketball and threw it into the hoop. "Is this what God wants me to do?"

◆ ◆ ◆

Milky put off cutting his yard that next Saturday. He had received a call from the auto shop where both he and Walter had their cars serviced, and they had a good friendship with the owner, Mr. Davis. After the accident, Milky asked him to look into how the accident might have happened, and asked him if he could provide him with a report. Mr. Davis went to the junk yard where the car had been towed. After a thorough inspection of the vehicle, Mr. Davis's report coincided with the insurance company's, which said Edna would not be eligible to file a claim for compensation of the car or wrongful death. There was no brake fluid in the car, and the brake pedal was loose. This surprised Mr. Davis because he had serviced the car just three months earlier. Nonetheless, because the car was old, anything could have happened in those three months. Milky thought it was best not to bother the family with this; they had endured enough grief. Mr. Davis agreed. "I also found some personal items in the car that I thought the family might want." Milky went that morning to pick up the items—a duffle bag containing some of Danny's clothes, some library books and the angel ornament that Lora gave Danny that Christmas to hang in his car.

◆ ◆ ◆

Lora and the girls did not go out to play tennis that Saturday, as it was still a time of mourning in the neighborhood. As she diced up chicken breast to go into the chicken pot pie she was preparing for Edna, her sister and Danny, the phone rang.

It was Frank. It had been nearly a month since they had spoken to each other—since their argument.

"I have had plenty of time to think, Lora, and I've read your letter over several times. We need to talk."

"I want to talk with you as well. I have missed you so much, and something tragic has happened. I called you on your beeper several times."

"I have been in Chicago, so my beeper probably could not pick up the signal. I just got back."

She went on to tell him about the accident. When she started to tell him about the grief and pain that Edna and Danny were feeling, he cut her off.

"You can finish telling me when I see you. When can that be?" Lora told him the next day, Sunday evening.

When the accident happened, Frank was on an early flight to Chicago. It was not to see his parents. Rather, it was to get away from Lora and away from the neighborhood. But while he was there, he did check on his parents to make sure their living will was the same—him as the sole beneficiary. He never stayed with his parents when he would visit. Rather he stayed at a hotel and enjoyed his favorite pastime—*making it rain*—in the bustling, progressive *Windy City* were strip joints were called strip *clubs* and considered *gentlemen's* entertainment.

Unbeknown to Lora, Frank already knew about the accident. He found about it from her boss a couple of days after it happened. He pretended to be calling about an order, but he really was fishing for information about Lora.

"Will the horticulturalist be able to have the pruning done in time for delivery?" inquired Frank.

"Well, we are a little bit behind. She had to take off a couple of days. A neighbor of hers died in a car accident. She's at home helping his wife and son."

"Son?"

"Yeah, can you imagine what that kid feels like, losing his father, especially right before his graduation?"

Frank was upset, but not because Walter had died. He was upset because he had hoped it had been Danny.

That Sunday after the girls retired, Frank arrived. Lora gave him more details about the accident and the funeral while he pretended to be sympathetic. She concluded by telling him that Danny would be going into the military. Lora also shared that Edna too may be leaving the neighborhood to go live with her sister.

Frank was quite pleased to hear this news, which made the proposal that he planned to make to her unnecessary. His proposal had been that she move out of the neighborhood—to a nicer place. He would help her find the place, and help with finances. Now, the only thing that he had to do was put up with Danny for a couple more months.

The rest of the evening was spent with Frank apologizing to Lora for not being with her during this troubled time, how much he missed her, how much her letter meant to him, that he did trust her, that he wanted to be with her and that he truly, truly loved her. Lora was so happy to have him hold and caress her that she did not have to go to sleep alone thinking about what happened to Walter.

They resumed their relationship and for the first time Frank was allowed to spend the night—that night and for the years to come.

CHAPTER XII

During the next ten years...

Big Lucy and Milky

Milky surprised Big Lucy on their 50th wedding anniversary by arranging a special party for her. In front of the 300 guests that were invited, he got down on his knees, and professed his love for her and how happy she had made him over the years. He also presented her with a diamond ring for her to wear in addition to the gold band he had given her 50 years ago. He then asked her if she would marry him again. Afterwards, he took her to Hawaii for a honeymoon—a place she always dreamed of going.

After retiring from the airport, Milky and Big Lucy volunteered full time at the homeless shelter, and worked to convince government officials to allocate more funding to open more shelters and programs to help homeless people get an education, jobs and resources to help them become self-sufficient. This was not an easy feat because government funding from all levels for such causes had been cut drastically during the 1980s. Milky and Big Lucy also recruited other volunteers to work at the shelters and hosted fundraisers on their own, generating thousands of dollars.

Their dedication, tireless efforts and accomplishments became recognized by people near and far. People with deep pockets started to join in their mission to help others, which got media coverage.

They received a letter from President Ronald Reagan, commending them and thanking them for their service to humanity. They had it framed and hung it over their fireplace, next to a photo of Big Lucy as a child with her mother, when they were homeless.

Edna

Edna moved to New Jersey to live with her sister. Felix rented her house for his niece, Tasha, who had moved from Jamaica with her three children. Felix made sure that they kept the property in pristine condition, and he paid Edna on time each month.

After about two years, Edna decided to stay in New Jersey and to sell the house. Felix bought it for his niece. Because Felix paid her cash and she did not have to pay a realtor commission, she made more money than she had expected. With the money, she bought a small townhouse within walking distance from her sister Erma.

Abah—her and Walter's childhood friend, who had become a wealthy man—paid for Edna and her sister to take a trip to the Motherland. The two ladies dressed in the traditional gowns and enjoyed feasting on the meals that the villagers had prepared in their honor, and enjoyed the tribal dancing and music that they remembered from their youth. However, the trip made Edna miss Walter even more.

Danny called his mother every week, sent her presents every holiday and for her birthday and sent her money every month.

Edna never got over the loss of Walter. She had grown completely gray in less than a year after his passing, and had lost her spunk and jovial disposition—lonely for her Walter.

Six years after Walter passed, Edna passed away as well. She died in her sleep. The doctor said it was an aneurism. Others felt it was from a broken heart.

Her body was flown back to Augusta, where she was buried next to Walter. Danny covered his mother's grave with the last scoop of dirt, just as he did when Walter was buried.

Mama J

Mama J's Saturday family visits now included 10 great grandchildren—four generations. She still cooked her collard greens, and often thought about Edna as she tried to flavor them as her dear friend liked.

Mr. Felix became Mama J's *special* friend. He attended church with her every Sunday along with his niece, Tasha, and her children, and they became part of her family gatherings.

Mama J and Mr. Felix often sat together reminiscing about the good times—laughing and filling their hearts with joy—as they sipped the sorrel that Mr. Felix would make. Mama J had acquired a taste for the sorrel which Mr. Felix made, occasionally spiking it with a wee bit of wine from the bottle that Lora gave to him before she left—the wine from her china cabinet—telling him it was for a "special occasion."

They missed Walter and Edna. "But we know they are with the Lord—in a better place," they reminded each other. "And Danny is doing well."

However, when they reminisced about Lora, the girls and Happy Go Lucky, there was only sadness as they remembered what happened at the little house in the middle of the cul-de-sac after Edna and Danny left the neighborhood.

Lora

Lora wanted to love Frank unconditionally. She did not want to lose another person whom she had loved, as was the case with Joseph and her adoptive parents.

Frank wanted more than Lora's love. Like Mama J would describe, "He wanted her soul in the way that the devil wanted Jesus's disciples."

Over the years, slowly and subtly, Frank made Lora submissive to his needs. He eroded her confidence in herself. He did this by persuasion, isolation, deceit and by making her insolvent.

He stalked her mind, starting with him stealing and making keys to her house and car. While she was at work, he would search all her belongings, looking for anything and everything to know about her. When he tried to open the drawers to the china cabinet and found them locked, he knew there had to be something important in them. His discerning and devious mind led him to the place were Lora hid the key. He read every single document—the insurance policies, her bank statements, the girl's education fund, her living will and the letter that Joseph had written to her.

When he read Joseph's letter, he knew now why she wanted him to take the AIDS test. But he was more concerned about obliterating any good memories she might have of the "faggot" so she wouldn't forgive Joseph, as was written in the letter. He tried to do this subtly by talking about men who were on the *down low*, and the women who had died because they contracted diseases from them.

When he read her living will, appointing Mama J as the girls' guardian, he was determined to break, or at least weaken, this bond. So he started telling Lora that she was putting too much of a burden on Mama J by always going over there, and reminded her that she was not her daughter and the girls were not her grandchildren. He even suggested that Mama J's kids were probably resentful of her for taking so much of her time, and probably jealous that Mama J was showing more affection to her girls than their children. While Lora did not believe these things, it became part of her subconscious, and doubted herself.

While Frank did not want to support Lora, he wanted her to be insolvent, needy, living from paycheck to paycheck. He wanted her to worry about how she could send the girls to college. He started telling Lora about investments plans. She felt that Frank was looking out for her best interest, and always admired his business sense and intellect. She trusted him, and gave him the liberty to re-invest her money. He purposefully invested her money in scams—including the girls' college funds.

More and more sinister things began to happen, as Lora was clueless of what Frank was doing to her, and Frank was becoming more and more powerful.

He would do things to make Lora nervous, feel unsafe and forgetful. He knew she was going to the store one night so he hid his car from view, sneaked up to her house, used the key that he made, unlocked her car and hid in the back seat. When Lora got into the dark car, he grabbed her neck from behind and put a knife to her throat. As she screamed with fright, he told her to relax, it was just him. He said he did it as a lesson to her that she should remember to lock her car. He often did things to make her think she was forgetful or negligent, such as turning the stove on after she turned

During The Next Ten Years...

it off, and misplacing or throwing away her mail—bills that were due.

He made her feel insecure about her job. He told her that when he spoke with her boss, the man would complain about the quality of her work. But he told her not to say anything because he would put in a good word on her behalf, and if the boss ever tried to fire her, he would threaten to pull the contract from the nursery. Consequently, she no longer felt relaxed at her job or at ease with her boss.

He knew that she was not a drinker, but he started to spike her non-alcoholic drinks with sedatives that would affect her judgment and memory. Often times, the sedatives would make her irritable once they wore off, which started to affect her relationship with the girls. And more often than not, they had to wait to talk with her until she was in a better mood. She seemed to lack energy, and rarely played tennis with them anymore. Frank liked seeing this— "You need to cut the umbilical cord," he would frequently say to Lora.

One day Happy Go Lucky disappeared, and despite a frantic search by Lora and the girls, he was nowhere to be found. Frank made Lora feel guilty by saying that she was negligent and shouldn't have a dog if she did not know how to care for it.

After seven years, Frank had Lora where he wanted her: penniless, unconfident, nervous, isolating herself from her neighbors, feeling guilty for what happened to Happy Go Lucky, addicted to sedatives, her girls avoiding her because of her irritable state of mind and feeling that he was the only one who cared about her. He felt that he had complete control over Lora and that he was paramount in her life. But the one thing that Frank could not alter, could not diminish, and what he underestimated, was the love that she had for her daughters.

While Frank had been oblivious of the girls when they were younger, as they grew older, he saw their significance. They exuded grace and confidence, were in the top of their class and had a refined beauty like their mother. But Veronica was the one he found most significant. While he found Cecilia more attractive because of her confident, vibrant personality and well-dressed style, he found Veronica's quiet nature and gentle demeanor more interesting. In two years, they would be graduating and leaving for college.

Veronica was home one morning, sick with the flu, when Frank came over. He heated up a can of chicken noodle soup and brought it to her. As she sipped on the soup, he felt her forehead to see if she had a fever. His hands started to roam their way down to her breasts. Without hesitation, Veronica threw the hot soup at Frank, who avoided the splash but could not avoid Veronica's wrath as she went after him, punching, scratching and kicking him with all her might. "Get away!" she screamed. "Get away!" Frank ran from the room and out of the house as Veronica hurled everything that she could throw at him. He sped off in his car. Veronica, crying and shaking, called her mother, "Mommy, come home, it's Frank—he tried to molest me!"

Lora immediately rushed home. After trying to comfort Veronica, she called the police, who took a report, but said because it was not an actual rape but a domestic dispute, they could not arrest Frank. They said they would file a report, which Lora would need if she wanted to follow up on the case with the District Attorney's office, if she wanted to prosecute.

Lora rushed to her car and sped over to Frank's Augusta apartment. He had packed some things and was leaving to go to his Atlanta condo. Lora pulled into the parking lot just as he was getting into his car. As she jumped out of her car and started running toward him, he hit the accelerator and pulled out of the parking space—almost hitting her. She kept running after him and screaming for him to stop, but then she tripped and fell face down on a large jagged boulder placed there for decoration. As Frank sped off, she lay unconscious and bleeding from the fall.

Lora woke up in the hospital, suffering from a concussion, a three-inch laceration on the right side of her forehead and a two-inch laceration on her face where her cheekbone was broken. Doctors told her that because she was prone to keloids—a form of scar tissue—most likely plastic surgery would not hide the scars.

In the case of the *State v. Frank Parker* for the crime of molestation of a minor, the jury found the defendant not guilty due to insufficient evidence. Frank tried to shake the hands of his high-priced attorneys but they snubbed him. They knew he was guilty, and this was why they had doubled their fees.

Two years later, the girls graduated from high school and headed to UCLA where they received scholarships for their tuition, and took out student loans to cover their cost of living. Lora sold the house to an investor who was looking for a good deal. She only netted about $8,000, all of which she sent to the girls. She took her antique vase and sold it for its full value—$3,500—and headed to Miami where she got a job at a nursery, thanks to the high recommendation she received from her boss. There, she found a furnished studio apartment that overlooked Biscayne Bay. It was more than she could afford, but the landlord said that if she would take care of the lawn and shrubs, he would reduce the rent.

Lora was ashamed of what happened in her life—for choosing a man like Frank—for not truly knowing him before she committed to him, as Joseph had advised. She felt that she had neglected her girls, and betrayed the loving friendship of her neighbors by not being honest and open with them about Frank. She wanted to get away from everything and everyone she had ever known. She felt the girls would be better off without her. She did not want to *feel* invisible as she did when she lived in New York—rather, she wanted to *be* invisible—never to be seen again. What put Lora into total despair was what she discovered when she was getting ready to move to Miami.

As she was packing and sorting things out in the garage for a Goodwill pick-up, she came across several large garbage bags containing clothing that the girls had outgrown. She started going through the bags to see what she might give to the Goodwill, and what should be thrown away. In one of the bags, instead of clothes, there was a broken tennis racket, a pair of rubber gloves covered in some sticky substance and some cloths with the same sticky substance. The smell and color of the substance was vaguely familiar to her. She sniffed it and suddenly it came to her—brake fluid. She recognized the smell from all the times she had poured it into her car. She again looked at the broken tennis racket, and recognized it as well—it was the tennis racket she had given to Danny.

"No, this can't be possible," she thought, as she realized Frank must have tampered with the brakes on Danny's car so many years earlier, causing the accident that killed Walter. She put the items into a cardboard box, sealed it and wrote on the front *For Danny*.

Before she left for Miami, she told Mama J everything that Frank had said and done to her.

However, she did not tell her about her suspicion of Frank killing Walter. She thought this would be too devastating for Mama J to bare, and she would not know what to do about it. Rather, she gave her the sealed up box for Danny, along with an envelope that contained a note that she had written to him. She told Mama J these items were for Danny's eyes only, this was very important, and to give them to him when she saw him again. While Lora had no faith in herself, she had faith in Mama J—that Mama J would see Danny again—and that Danny would know what to do about the contents in the box.

Mama J never heard from Lora after that. But she always heard from the girls, who told her Lora was doing okay, and that she was content with her life in Miami.

Cecilia and Veronica

While Lora had lost all confidence in herself, Cecilia's and Veronica's confidence in her, and the love and admiration for their mother, never wavered.

As they packed for college, they reminisced in their room with the purple curtains, glitter ceiling and yellow door that was so full of memories. They laughed as they looked at some of the things they wore as kids. The costumes that their mother made for Halloween—when Cecilia was the good witch and Veronica the good fairy, and they tied

During The Next Ten Years...

for first place in the school's costume contest. The outfits that they wore to church—looking like miniature versions of Mama J— "a Mama J mini-me" they would say. The dresses that Lora stayed up all night making so that they would be the envy at prom—and they were.

As they packed their photo albums, they reminisced about their neighbors: how much fun they had at Mama J's family gatherings; the sleepovers at Ms. Edna's; how Ms. Lucy and Mr. Milky taught them to care for the unfortunate. They remembered Danny—the fun they had on the trampoline, the card tricks he taught them, their trip to Disney World and how they wanted him to be their uncle. And they thought about Happy Go Lucky as they packed the framed photos of him—where could he have possibly gone? Mama J would always comfort them by saying that dogs had souls and do go to heaven.

They also remembered the day when their mother told them about their father. When they were younger, she showed them pictures and told him he died from a virus. They thought their father was quite handsome, as did Lora. Lora also told them about how they met, and how they fell in love. But when they were 16, Lora told them the truth, and let them read the letter. The girls were both deeply saddened. But they were not ashamed of him; rather they felt a deep compassion for how he died and the pain and remorse he felt.

Both girls made a copy of the photo that was taken when they were two, with their father and mother, and had it framed to hang in their dorm room. The also made copies of Joseph's letter asking God to protect them, and that they always had angels by their side.

"We have had angels by our side," Cecilia said to Veronica as she thought about the neighbors and Danny.

"And the Devil tried to take them away," Veronica said as she thought about Frank.

Frank

Both of Frank's parents passed away, just two years apart. They left him nothing. All their money, plus a mortgage they took on their house, went to pay for their medical bills and an expensive rest home. But what they did leave Frank was some bad genes. Both died from diabetes, which Frank found out he was also afflicted with. The disease was now taking a toll on his body and the doctor said most likely his legs would eventually have to be amputated. Also, his vision was bad — glaucoma in one eye, cataract in the other, and he was already near-sighted. Frank was a medical mess, and his body was now as sick as his evil mind.

And so was his business. He was unable to keep tabs on the finances and contract negotiations

During The Next Ten Years...

because of his failing health. The company was now in the red, and he was being audited by the IRS.

He sold his Atlanta condo, which netted only a small profit because of the principal he owed, the realtor's commission, bank fees and closing costs. He still was not destitute enough to receive disability. Thanks to his medical plan that was underwritten by the business, his medical bills were covered.

Frank felt no remorse for what he had done to Lora. He was only sorry that he had to pay all those attorney fees to get him off the hook for trying to molest Veronica. "Heck, I didn't even get to first base."

He also felt no remorse for what happened to Walter. Rather, he felt what a waste of time it had been, since it was Danny whom he intended to kill. All the trouble that he went through was wasted.

Frank knew that the neighbors did not lock their cars from his conversation with Lora when he reprimanded her for not locking her car. She told him that no one locked their cars because they felt safe in the neighborhood with the hood rats now cleared out of the nearby neighborhoods. So Frank set about enacting his treacherous plan. He knew Lora would be fast asleep that night from the sedatives. In the pitch black of night, Frank went over to the carport where Danny's car was parked. He turned on his flashlight, careful that it didn't shine where someone could see him. He sopped out all the brake fluid from the car with a rag, and loosened the brake pedal. He also saw Danny's tennis racket in the back seat, and viciously he cut the strings to shreds. When he was finished, he put the racket and the automotive waste in a trash bag and left it in Lora's shed with another pile of trash bags, which he assumed would be picked up soon by the trash collectors.

Although he failed to get rid of Danny, when Lora told him Danny would be going into the military, Frank was satisfied. "Too bad for the old man—but that's what happens when you have kids. You always have to sacrifice yourself for them." Frank felt victorious.

But even with Danny gone, Frank was not satisfied. Even with Lora professing her love to him and devoting all her spare time to him, he was not satisfied. The only thing that really satisfied Frank was seeing Lora in a helpless state, one that he could manipulate and control.

Although he would not, and could not, ever be with Lora again because of what he did to Veronica, he felt satisfied thinking that she would never, ever forget him. "Every time she looks at those scars on her face, she will think of me," he thought. As it had many times before, his power over her inflated his ego and aroused him sexually.

Danny

During Danny's training as a medic in the Marines he had seen bodies that had been blown apart. In the mobile medical units, with bare necessities, he learned to patch up bodies that seemed beyond repair—reattaching limbs, putting organs and guts back into body cavities, icing and bandaging bodies that were burned from head to toe, trying to save what was left of a face that was no longer recognizable. No matter how severe the injuries, as long as there was a sign of life, medics did not give up on trying to save the wounded. These lives not only included his fellow marines, but innocent children and villagers who were victims of the wars, including the Gulf War, the Lebanon War and covert missions in South America, Africa and the Middle East.

While Danny learned how to save lives, he was also trained in combat—to kill—to take out a life not only with one shot of a rifle, but also with a split second twist of the neck, a finger to crush a crucial artery or a karate kick that would decapitate a head.

It had been 10 years, and Danny, because of his military duty, had only been back to Augusta once and that was to bury his mother. He had done his time to serve his country. He was now coming home to formally attend medical school. He wanted to get the credentials needed to join Doctors Without Borders and help children who had disfigurements in countries that lacked medical care. Harvard Medical School had accepted his application and gave him credit him for his military experience as a medic. It would take him only four years to become a certified medical doctor. He was scheduled to start that fall, which gave him a few weeks to visit his old neighborhood, and put flowers on his parents' grave.

While visiting their gravesite, he told Walter and Edna about his plans. "I'll get that Harvard degree, I promise you. And I am going to hang it next to your picture—the one you took with me when I was born," he promised them. He then headed to his old neighborhood.

As he drove, passing through neighborhoods, he thought about how blessed Americans were to live in a country where they did not have to listen to gun fire and exploding bombs day and night. As he passed a playground, looking at the children, he though how fortunate they were to not have to play in dirt and sand fields and get blown up by grenades that were hidden in the dirt.

After Edna died, he didn't hear too much about the neighborhood. His Aunt Erma did tell him, however, that Lora had moved. "Heard that the pretty little lady with the twins moved, and something happened over there to make her move away, but I didn't get no details," she shared. Her main source of information had been Mr. Felix, whom she became acquainted with while renting and selling Edna's house. But Mr. Felix did not talk very much, especially about his neighbors' business.

It was evident to Danny that Lora had moved as he pulled into the cul-de-sac. The house was still sitting there, vacant once again, as the investor waited for the market to go up before putting it up for sale. It now looked like it did when Lora first moved in—dilapidated with weeds that had grown as tall as sugar cane.

While at the florists getting flowers for his parents' gravesite, he also purchased a vase of red roses for Mama J, and one with yellow roses for Ms. Lucy. For Milky, he brought a cap with a Marine's insignia.

"Oh, my Jesus!" Mama J hollered when she opened the door. Danny almost dropped the vase of roses as she wrapped him in a surprisingly powerful embrace, given her age. "What a fine looking man," she thought, as he had grown even taller and much more muscular, looking so much like Walter.

Big Lucy heard Mama J cry out "Oh, my Jesus," dropped the dish she was washing, and ran to the window. "Danny!" she hollered, as she ran out barefooted, her hands dripping from the dish water, and hugged him. After the hugs, Big Lucy went back home, put on some shoes and called Milky to tell him Danny was home. She hurried back to Mama J's.

The rest of the afternoon they spent talking. Danny answered their question about the military, leaving out all the gory details—making it sound instead like an episode of *M.A.S.H.* However, all he wanted was to hear about them—how they were doing. Most of all he wanted to know about Lora and the girls. And surely he did hear, as the conversation went well into the evening. Milky brought home some Kentucky Fried Chicken so the ladies would not have to cook, and Mama J was an hour late to her appointment with Jesus and to read her Bible.

The ladies insisted that Danny spend the night, but he convinced them he needed to get back to his hotel, since he had no change of clothes. He promised that he would come back soon. But the real reason he wanted to leave was because he needed to internalize what they had told him about what had happened to Lora and the girls. Mama J told him everything she'd seen Frank do to her, and the disfigurement of her face.

As he was about to leave, Mama J gave him the box and envelope that Lora had told her to give to him. "I don't know what it is, but she said it was very personal." He asked her if she had Lora's contact information—phone number, address. Mama J said no, only that she lived somewhere in Miami, but she did have the girls' contact information.

As Danny was leaving, and the ladies following him out to his car to say goodbye, he looked over at the house he remembered so fondly and asked, "What happened to the mahogany door?"

During The Next Ten Years...

Mama J answered. "The day that Lora left, she beat it with a sledge hammer until it fell apart. Don't know why."

◆ ◆ ◆

When Danny got back to the hotel, he made a call. "Gloria, I need you to find the addresses of two people.... Lora Jones, date of birth November 10, 1950, Miami, Florida. I need her telephone number as well—it's probably unlisted, but you know how to get it. I also need the address of Frank Parker, somewhere in Augusta or Atlanta, Georgia. I don't have a birthdate, but he's somewhere in his mid to late 40s. I need this information no later than tomorrow, as early as possible. Thanks." Gloria worked in special investigations for the military.

He then opened the envelope and read Lora's note. Its brevity was because she could not find the words to express how guilty she felt, and how Danny was going to resent her for what happened—that if she had not chosen to be with Frank, his father would be alive.

> *My Dearest Danny,*
>
> *My heart aches with pain as I write this—so badly that I cannot express what I feel. I know that what you are going to find in this box is going to hurt you deeply, but I owe you the truth. I found the contents of this box in my shed as I was moving. I think it is evidence that Frank*

caused your father's death by tampering with the brakes. He had meant to kill you because he was jealous of you, of our innocent relationship. But it is my fault because I chose to be with a man so evil. I hope you will find it in your heart to forgive me, and pray that your parents, who are in heaven, will forgive me also.

Love, Lora

Danny opened the box and inspected its contents. He went into military combat mode—to kill without mercy or remorse an enemy that does not deserve to live.

Gloria called Danny early the next morning with the information he needed. He strapped on the holster with his handgun and headed out to Frank's place.

Approaching the house, he took out the gun and released the safety mechanism and kicked open the door. He heard Frank cry out, "Who's that!"

Danny quickly scanned the house and saw no one else was there. He proceeded to the bedroom, where Frank was scrambling to get to his phone. Danny kicked it out of his hand just as Frank was about to dial 911. Frank squinted his eyes, as he needed his glasses to make out the face of the tall dark figure in front of him holding the gun.

"Don't shoot, don't kill me! Take whatever you want!" Frank screamed and pleaded as Danny yanked the covers off him. He saw Frank's decaying feet and legs and realized he had a severe case of diabetes, as Frank was whimpering and begging for his life. On the dresser, he saw Frank's glasses with thick lenses, and seeing him squinting, realized that he also had a serious vision problem.

Danny now contemplated how he should kill Frank—to snap his neck or pinch off an artery. Frank was now urinating all over himself and diarrhea was seeping out from under him, while he was still whimpering and pleading, "Don't kill me!" Danny had absolutely no pity for him, and badly wanted to end Frank's worthless life. But then Danny realized that if he did kill him, it would only put Frank out of his misery—that he would in fact be doing Frank a favor.

That urge to kill Frank was still pulsating within every fiber of Danny's body—revenge for his father, for Lora, for Veronica. He was not afraid of being convicted for murdering Frank. He was smart enough to know how to do it without becoming a suspect. Neither was he going to go through the judicial system to have Frank convicted for killing his father. He knew that because of the time that had lapsed and the circumstantial evidence, Frank would probably get off scot-free.

And then Danny realized what would truly hurt Frank—more than the pain from his diabetes. But like diabetes, it would make him suffer until the day he died. He handed Frank his glasses, and told him to put them on. Frank, shaking like a leaf, put them on. Recognizing the figure before him, he hollered out with even greater fear as if he had seen a ghost.

"Oh shit, you're Walter! No, no, no, you're Danny! Oh, please, please, I didn't mean it! I didn't mean to kill your father! I meant to kill—"

"Me?" Danny asked as he approached the bed so Frank could hear him click the gun to fire mode.

"Yes, no, I meant no! I didn't mean to kill nobody! Please, please don't kill me!"

"But my wife said that I must kill you for what you did to her."

"Your wife?"

"Yes, Lora, Lora my wife."

Suddenly, the old Frank came back as he looked at Danny with hate. It was the look that Danny wanted to see—the look that gave Danny the revenge he needed. Danny said no more, but just turned and walked away, leaving Frank's ego more crippled than his body, and who would live in fear wondering if Danny would come back.

As Danny was leaving, he put his gun into safety mode and back into his holster. He also turned off the pocket-sized recorder that he had in his pocket that tape recorded Frank admitting he killed Walter. Just as he opened the front door, he heard a sound—a soft yelp. He turned around and saw in a corner of the dirty, dark room, smelling of urine and feces, a mangy little dog. Looking closer, he felt he knew the poor little dog, and the dog seemed to know him as it started to wag its wretched tail. "Gimme your paw," he said. The little dog obeyed and Danny shook its paw. It was Happy Go Lucky "Hey, boy, you remember me? It's me, Danny." Happy Go Lucky wagged his tail with all his might, and licked Danny's face.

Danny hurriedly took him to the nearest animal hospital. The veterinarian said that Happy Go Lucky was full of fleas and malnourished, but basically healthy. And even though he was well up in his age, with some TLC, he'd be just fine. The vet wrote down the names of vitamins and high protein food that he recommended. After the exam, an attendant took Happy Go Lucky to the grooming area to get a bath, teeth brushed, ears cleaned, claws trimmed and fur brushed. In the meantime, Danny went to a nearby pet store and bought the items the vet recommended, as well as a dog collar and leash and a box of doggie cookies.

The next morning, Danny and Happy Go Lucky hit the highway and headed out to Miami.

Danny & Lora

Danny cruised the highway until he came to the sign that said *Welcome to Florida* and then *Miami 180 miles*. He exited at the next rest stop to stretch his legs and for Happy Go Lucky to stretch his, and for both of them to take a leak. He knew too that he should call Lora, to ask her if she wanted to see him, and went to the phone booth. Then he thought maybe he should not call her—just show up—so that she would not have the opportunity to decline his visit. But that would be inconsiderate on his part and he felt ashamed for even thinking it. Even if she did say no, his purpose would not be in vain because he was sure she would want to see Happy Go Lucky. He would simply leave Happy Go Lucky in front of her door, attaching the leash to the doorknob.

The phone rang several times with no answer, so he decided to hang up. Just as he was about to put the receiver back into its cradle, he heard her voice. "Hello?"

His voice choked up and he tried to clear it. "Hello, Mrs. Jones, this is Danny, Danny Ayoka."

"Oh my God, Danny, it's you, where are you?" Lora said in a voice that convinced Danny that she was glad to hear from him.

He told her he was in Florida, headed to Miami, and asked if he could come see her. She said she would love to see him. Then it dawned on her, and him as well, that if he knew she was in Miami, he had spoken with Mama J, who told him everything and had given him the package. There was silence as both of them thought about what to say next. Danny broke the silence.

"Mama J told me everything, and I got the package and letter you wrote to me. I just want to see you, to know that you are alright. Are you sure you want to see me?"

"Of course. Here's my address. Do you have something to write it down?" He took the address even though he had it already. He did not want to explain to her—complicate things—by telling her how he got it. He told her that he was about three hours away.

Lora took a shower and changed to into a floral sundress. She rarely looked into the mirror anymore, but forced herself to now as she wanted to look her best for Danny. She got out some concealer makeup to try to cover the scars, but she could not conceal the keloid tissue. She then looked at herself with disgust in the mirror. "Here I am worrying about what he is going to think about my scars. Instead I should be thinking about what he'll think about me for getting his father killed." She looked at herself again in the mirror, wiped off the makeup and said to the face in the mirror, "You deserve these scars!"

Lora then had second thoughts about seeing Danny. Her purpose for moving to Miami was to erase her past and avoid all contact with those she had disappointed. She even avoided seeing the girls, and had not seen them since they moved away to college. She would talk with them on the phone, but when they asked about visiting, she'd convince them it was too costly, and that they should concentrate on their studies. All the time that she had been living in Miami, she had not cultivated any friends, and lived in solitude. But then she thought she needed to see Danny—to tell him in person how bad she felt about what happened to Walter. It was something she needed to have the courage to do, even though she had no courage to do anything else in her life.

She figured Danny would be hungry so she pulled out the delivery menus and decided to order some Chinese food. As she thought about what to order, Danny called again and asked if he could bring some food, and if she liked Chinese.

"I was just about to order Chinese!" she exclaimed. They both laughed, and he said he was at the restaurant now, and should be at her place in about 20 minutes.

"Okay, now wouldn't it be ironic if he ordered what I would have—pork fried rice, cashew chicken, broccoli and dumpling soup?" Lora thought.

Lora was speechless when she opened the door. He no longer looked like a boy—a growing teenager. She had always imagined that he would grow up to be a strappingly handsome man. But there was something about his whole physical makeup that in her eyes made him look almost saintly.

"You look great, Danny, come on in," she said as she led him to the kitchenette.

"So do you, Mrs. Jones," he replied.

"Don't lie to me, Danny—I got a mirror. I know what I look like," she said gently but without sounding as if she were feeling sorry for herself.

During The Next Ten Years...

To Danny, she was still beautiful—despite the scars, and he had seen far worse while in the military. But he wasn't going to try to convince her, at least not right now. "There's paper plates, forks, chopsticks in there as well," he said as Lora started to unpack the food. Lora, smiled as she remembered the first time she met Danny—when he brought over the paper plates that the ladies forgot to bring when they came over with dinner to welcome her to the neighborhood.

"Mrs. Jones, I have something else in the car for you. I'll be right back," Danny said as he went back to the car to get Happy Go Lucky.

While he was gone, Lora prepared the plates. "Well, I'll be a monkey's uncle, he got three out four right," she said as she looked at the food he ordered.

"It's open," Lora called out as Danny rang the doorbell holding Lora's precious surprise. She cupped her hands over her mouth, and just stood there speechless, thinking that her eyes were betraying her. Happy Go Lucky started yelping and trying to get out of Danny's arms to get to Lora. Danny bent down and let him run into the arms of Lora, who fell to her knees and hugged the dog that lived up to his name.

As they ate and talked, Danny tried to address what he knew troubled her. He assured Lora that what happened to his father was not her fault. He told her about his trip to Frank's place, that he was pathetic and not worth their time for revenge or even anger. He told her about Frank's health condition and that he was doomed to die a painful, agonizing death soon. He told her how he found Happy Go Lucky there, and what the vet said—to give him plenty of TLC and he would be fine.

This gave way to the rest of the evening with delightful conversation. Lora told Danny about how well the girls were doing in college and that she hoped he would get in touch with them. He said he intended to. He told her that being in the military was a blessing in spite of seeing the horrors of war, and that his years of service and training qualified him to attend Harvard to get his medical degree. He told her the neighbors were just fine, and that Mama J was as fit as a fine-tuned fiddle and Mr. Felix was her boyfriend.

Lora could see that Danny was curious about all the boxes stacked up in by her front door, and the bareness of her place. So she told him that she was packing things up to send to California. He said he thought it would be good if she lived closer to her daughters and he asked her when she was planning to leave. She told him in a couple of days, that he had caught her just in time. He asked her if she needed any help—financially or otherwise. She said she was just fine. He said if she ever needed any help, for anything, anyway, that she could count on him. He told her that his main concern was to know that she was happy. He could tell she was not. It was something in her eyes—a look that he saw in his mother's eyes ever since his father died. It was a look that he saw as a medic when soldiers had become disabled and no longer wanted to live.

"Mrs. Jones, you are still a beautiful woman, and you need to feel that," he told her. "Those scars can be removed, and the keloids. Trust me. When you are ready, I will arrange for it. I will be in the operating room to make it happen. But what is more important is that you erase the scars in your heart. Only you can do that."

There was so much more they wanted to say to one another, but to do so, it would take away the innocence — the purity — of their relationship.

It was time to say goodbye. Lora reached up and gave him a gentle kiss on his cheek. And for the first time he gave her a kiss, first on the scar on her forehead, and then a kiss on the scar on her cheek. He wanted so badly to kiss her on her yearning lips. But that would not be right.

Once more he felt the butterflies fluttering in his stomach — a sensation that no else would ever be able to make him feel again.

Farewell

All of Lora's boxes were nearly packed and labeled for delivery to her daughters. She filled a bowl with the dog food that Danny had bought from the vet, and packed the rest, marking the box *Food for Happy Go Lucky*.

She picked up the journal that Danny had given her that Christmas long ago, with her name inscribed on the cover. It only had one entry—the entry that she had made when she got the call from the hospital about Joseph. That night, she filled the rest of the pages with thoughts about her daughters, her loving neighbors and Danny. She wrote her last entry:

Dear God,

Thank you for all that you have given me. Please forgive me for all my mistakes, for making wrong choices that have caused others pain. Please ask Walter to forgive me. Please tell Joseph that his girls love him. Please take care of my neighbors, Danny and my girls.

She closed the journal and put it in the box to be shipped with important papers, photos and keepsakes that she wanted her girls to have.

The following day, UPS picked everything up, and the driver assured her the boxes would arrive in two days, since she was sending them priority express. Then she went to the travel agency and purchased a ticket for Happy Go Lucky to fly to California, and found a nearby store to purchase a dog crate. When she returned to her studio, she called the landlord. He and his wife tried to befriend Lora when she first came to Miami, somewhat like her loving neighbors did when she lived in Augusta.

But Lora kept her distance. She asked her landlord if he would do her a favor. She explained to him that she had a little dog that needed to go to California, but that he could not go with her. She had a crate and airline ticket for him, but needed someone to take him to the airport at noon the next day; would he do her this favor? He said it would be no problem.

Early the next morning, she could tell that Happy Go Lucky needed to urgently relieve himself, and because of his age, he could not hold on too long. So, rather than making him wait until she could take him for a walk, she opened the back patio door to her balcony that faced Biscayne Bay. He let go, feeling the breeze of the outdoors. She then gave him some of the doggie cookies that she had not packed. "Yes, boy, you're going to California, and the girls will be so happy to see you," she said to him as she hugged him.

It was almost 9:00 am. She called the girls, who were now living together in off-campus housing at UCLA. She knew they would not be home because they had early morning classes, but she left a message on their answering machine. She told them to expect boxes from UPS in a couple of days. She also told them they needed to pick up Happy Go Lucky from the airport at 6:00 pm their time. She said she could not explain this turn of events, but to call Danny who would explain, and she gave them his number.

As she hung up, she again thought about Danny—his wing span—her angel on earth with the biggest wing span ever. Her feelings for him were no longer pure, and her love could not be denied if she were ever to see him again.

After giving Happy Go Lucky another hug and doggie cookie, she picked up the box with Joseph's ashes, and walked barefooted to Biscayne Bay. It was a windy day, and she was sure Joseph's ashes would make their way to Jamaica as she tilted the box and they blew away in the easterly wind.

She then walked out into the water to meet the approaching wave that would take her away into the deep blue ocean—that would take away all the pain in her heart, her remorse, her guilt, her loneliness and a love in her heart that could never be.

Through the roaring of the approaching wave that would take her away, she heard yelping. It was Happy Go Lucky, sitting on her balcony, looking at her, calling and begging her to come back.

The End

EPILOGUE

While laws have been enacted to protect victims of physical abuse and stalking, there are no laws protecting one from mental abuse and stalking of the mind, as portrayed in this novel. *The Story of Lora* is about only one victim. Millions of victims' stories are never told.

Dear Readers:

When I retired, I decided to fulfill a long time dream which was to write a novel. Many who know me said it was a calling—a gift for story writing.

My greatest challenge was that I did not know what I wanted to write about. But one day I woke up and the character was in my head—*Lora*. From that morning on, she spoke to me about her life. There were days when she was reluctant to talk with me, but I persisted. And there were days when I did not understand her, but I was patient. After she finished telling me her story, I knew it was a story that others would want to hear. While she is a fictional character, she represents those whose stories are never told.

I hope you will enjoy *The Story of Lora* as much as I enjoyed writing it. After reading, please share your thoughts with me on my website. Thank you!

Yvonne Smith James
The Story of Lora

POST A REVIEW

www.StoryofLora.com